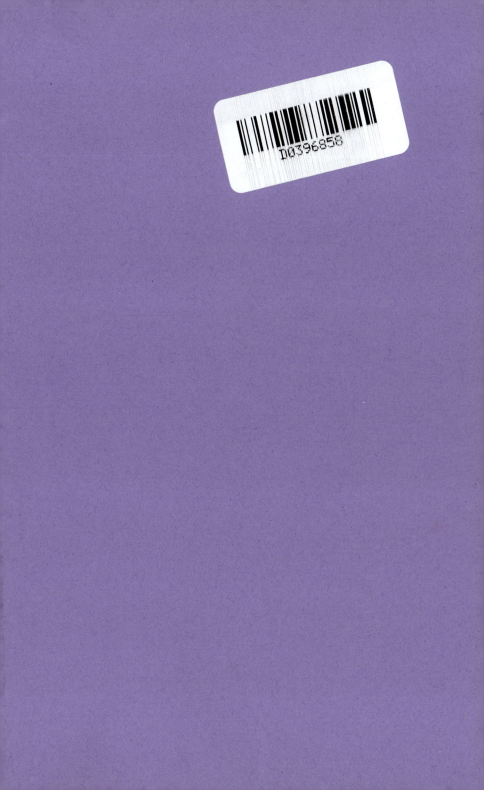

Kazu Jones

AND THE
DENVER DOGNAPPERS

by SHAUNA HOLYOAK

Disney • HYPERION

Los Angeles   New York

First Edition, April 2019
10 9 8 7 6 5 4 3 2 1
FAC-020093-19067
Printed in the United States of America

This book is set in New Caledonia LT Std / Adobe; Aspirin ITC Std /
International; Arian LT / Monotype
Designed by Mary Claire Cruz
Illustrations by Grace Hwang

Library of Congress Cataloging-in-Publication Data

Names: Holyoak, Shauna M., author
Title: Kazu Jones and the Denver dognappers / by Shauna M. Holyoak.
Description: First edition. • Los Angeles ; New York : Disney/
Hyperion, 2019.
• Summary: Eleven-year-old Kazuko, already well-known for "helping" the
police, investigates a rash of dognappings, aided by her Japanese mastiff,
Genki, and friends.
Identifiers: LCCN 2018030257• ISBN 9781368022408 (hardcover) • ISBN
9781368022668 (pbk.)
Subjects: • CYAC: Mystery and detective stories. • Dogs—Fiction. •
Stealing—Fiction. • Japanese Americans—Fiction. • Family
life—Colorado—Denver—Fiction. • Denver (Colo.)—Fiction.
Classification: LCC PZ7.1.H6515 Kaz 2019 • DDC [Fic]—dc23
LC record available at https://lccn.loc.gov/2018030257

Reinforced binding

Visit www.DisneyBooks.com

SUSTAINABLE FORESTRY INITIATIVE   Certified Sourcing
www.sfiprogram.org
SFI-00993

THIS LABEL APPLIES TO TEXT STOCK

To my husband, Mike—
my champion, best friend, and lobster

CHAPTER ONE

Mom let me keep my paper route even though there was a dognapper on the loose. It was a tough sell, but I convinced her I was a ganbariya, with the spunk to slog through the mud pits of life.

Mom was distracted by my clever Japanese skills and didn't suspect a thing about my detective work. It was *always* about the detective work.

But even girl detectives with ginormous watchdogs named Genki got nervous about dognappers roaming their town before sunrise. So when I delivered papers, I rode my bike fast and kept my eyes open for suspicious characters.

This morning I stood on the pedals of my baby-blue Schwinn cruiser as I turned the corner at the end of my block, the crunching gravel under my wheels loud in the still streets. Genki ran beside me, nearly as tall as the bike. Dad had trained him to be my slobbery bodyguard, and there was no place I could go that Genki wouldn't shadow me.

My basket was packed with rolled newspapers, and they caught air each time my bike jumped the curb or hit a rock. Like always, I had pulled my sneakers on without tying them, and the laces wagged in the wind.

At dawn, the fall sky in Denver, Colorado, was the color of purple velvet, and the air smelled like wet dirt and smoke, probably from people using their fireplaces for the first time. No one turned their porch lights on this soon after summer, so the streets were crowded with dark shadows.

I cycled with my head down, pumping so fast my feet nearly spun off the pedals. As I neared the corner house, where a kitchen light glowed like the Bat-Signal, I noticed movement in the back garden. Genki's head snapped to attention.

I slowed down, and Genki's gallop turned to a trot as my bike hugged the curb. We both watched as a shadowy figure shuffled around the garden, pausing to hunch over a pile of dirt. I squinted past the squat trees surrounding the yard that looked like soldiers standing guard. I could just barely see the person drag something heavy into a hole, followed by a loud "Oomph!"

I swung my leg over the crossbar. Genki matched my steps and studied my face as I rested the bike gently against the sidewalk. We hid behind a tree.

The suspicious character wore a dark robe and walked like a hunchbacked monster. As if savoring each moment, it began to fill the hole with a miniature shovel. It had to be burying a body, probably one of the dogs that had been snatched by Denver's Dognapping Ring—nearly fifteen dogs had disappeared over the summer.

Genki leaned into me as I knelt, his whining a low and practically soundless vibration in his chest. Even though he was a big dog—a mastiff—he had a social anxiety disorder. At least, that's what Mom said.

As I peeked around the tree trunk, my elbow knocked over a metal rooster that decorated the lawn, and it clattered like a tin-can tower tumbling to the ground. The hunchbacked monster's head snapped up, a halo of hair frizzing in the kitchen light. I jumped and Genki barked.

I darted across the lawn and stood my bike upright before running it alongside me, Genki trotting behind. When I turned onto Colonial Avenue, I let it go. It wobbled a few feet and then crashed in front of my BFF March Winters's house, the newspapers in my basket exploding onto the road.

Scooping an armful, I ran to March's window—the last one on the second floor—and began chucking papers.

They thudded against the house, missing his window wildly, but his light flicked on anyway. March was always the first to wake up in the Winterses' house, rising as soon as his alarm went off at six thirty. *Show-off.*

He strained to open the window and then shook his head when he recognized me. "What are you doing here this early, Kazu?" he whispered.

"You need to call the police," I whispered back. "Your neighbor is a criminal."

March rolled his eyes. His springy dark hair was flat on one side from sleeping. "I'm not calling the police."

"Well, I can't do it." I looked over my shoulder for the Hunchbacked Monster but just found Genki plopping down behind me and licking his front paws. "On account of they don't take my calls anymore."

"Why should I join that list?"

"Because there's someone burying a dog over there." I pointed across the street with a shaky finger.

Suddenly March's alarm blared, and he disappeared from the window. I crouched on his lawn and began collecting the rolled newspapers around me, watching for the Denver Dognapper as I worked. Genki became interested in my movements and pounced on each paper before I could pick it up.

"Stop it!" I snapped, and Genki finally stopped.

"You saw it?" March reappeared in the golden light of his window frame. "My neighbor, burying a dog?"

4

I stood with my newspapers. "Probably one of Denver's Missing."

He sighed and folded his arms across his chest, tapping his elbow with his pointer finger. "I'll call. But you stay until the police get here—in case you're wrong."

"Do you not know me?" The sun was coming up, and the new light made me brave. I stopped whispering. "When would *I* skip out on an investigation?"

"Stay right there," he said. "I'll unlock the front door."

I sat on March's curb while Mom talked to the policeman and Eleanor Fitzman, the old lady who lived kitty-corner from March. Genki leaned into me, breathing into my ear and getting slobber on my shoulder.

Mrs. Fitzman bent over her cane while she talked to Officer Perks. She was wearing a navy-blue bathrobe and had Einstein hair. The policeman glared at me from over her head, twice as tall as Mrs. Fitzman, his hair black and curly. He looked like an ordinary guy dressed in a policeman costume.

Mrs. Fitzman held one hand to her neck as she spoke. "Mister Mapples had been with me for fifteen years, which is long for a pug. And that's five years longer than Hank now," she said. She looked at Mom, adding, "Mr. Fitzman passed five years ago."

Mom nodded dramatically, as if her rapt attention made up for my dognapping accusations.

As the old lady explained the slow decline of her now-dead husband, I rested my head on my knees, looking up the street at all the houses still waiting for their newspapers. At the corner house I caught an old guy watching us, his upper body leaning over a garbage can. I craned my neck to get a better look, and he turned around, pulling the garbage can behind him.

Mrs. Fitzman was still talking. "When I awoke this morning—early because of the insomnia—Mister Mapples was gone. I couldn't bear to sit with his lifeless body one minute more, so I buried him in the flower patch." We all knew this was true because she had unburied him for us ten minutes ago, and then shuffled inside to locate the doggie adoption certificate and a framed photograph as proof that Mister Mapples was indeed her dead dog.

Officer Perks looked like he was competing in the Most Bored Person on the Planet Contest. He pretended to take notes. Mom cinched her cotton robe tighter, stole a glance my way, and narrowed her eyes at me, deepening the crease between her brows.

"I'm so sorry Kazuko disturbed you this morning," Mom said, motioning me over. Even though she had left the house in a hurry, her black hair was slick and perfectly straight.

I stood and walked toward them, shoving my hands deep into my jacket pockets. Genki followed, hanging his head like he knew we were in trouble.

"I'm sorry," I said.

"Oh, sweetie," Mrs. Fitzman said. She reached out and grabbed my hand. Her palm was soft and fleshy, and the dirt smiling beneath her fingernails made me like her. "You performed your civic duty. With all the dogs disappearing, you had every reason to be suspicious. Right, Officer Perks?"

Officer Perks hesitated before responding. "Kazuko is known for her passionate pursuit of truth and justice."

Mom nodded as Officer Perks repeated, "*Well* known."

"Then," Mrs. Fitzman said, tapping her cane to each word, "good for you."

I smiled, but stopped when Mom's face hardened, her jawline suddenly pointy and dangerous.

"Kazuko will be late for school if we don't hurry. And I still have to finish her route," Mom said, squeezing my hand knuckle-tight as she did. She wasn't happy about doing my job when she still had her own to do. She was designing a new exhibit for the Denver Exploration Museum for Kids. "My apologies, Officer Perks. And, Mrs. Fitzman, I'm sorry for your loss."

The policeman stepped forward and grabbed my elbow to stop me. "Your dog is off its leash." With all the dognappings, the city had gotten pretty strict about leash laws.

I shrugged. "He's really good about following me."

Officer Perks scratched something down on his pad and then ripped it off with flair. I took it from him and read, *Loose dog warning. Next time, maximum penalty. Signed, Officer Warren Perks.* I folded the paper into a tiny square and shoved it into my pocket, pinching my lips together so I wouldn't say anything.

Mom and I walked to the car, which was parked in front of the Winterses' house. To all the neighbors peeking from behind their curtains, it probably looked like a loving mother was guiding her daughter to the car with a gentle hand pressed to her back. But actually, Mom's fingers drilled into my spine, and under her breath she rattled off stinging threats about extra chores and reduced screen times that continued as we drove down the street.

Genki lay across my lap, his whining echoing inside the car. "It's okay, pup pup." I scratched his ears to make the social anxiety go away.

"This troublemaking binge has got to stop, Kazuko Jones." Mom drummed her fingers on the steering wheel. "What happened to my sweet girl who was all about crafts and swimming lessons and lunch dates with Mom?"

"I'm nearly eleven and one-quarter," I said, unable to stop myself. "Not seven."

Mom's lecture continued as we turned onto Summer Glen, and I distracted myself by studying the house where I had seen the old man earlier. It was one of *my* houses, and the spookiest one on my route. Dark brown and barely visible from the road, it was shrouded by fir trees and gave me the creeps. And as we passed, I could have sworn I saw someone peeking at us through the blinds in the corner window.

CHAPTER TWO

I'm grounded from you again," March said as I slid next to him on the bus. We always sat on the last bench by the emergency exit, where no one bugged us because we were fifth graders.

"How long this time?" I pulled my Sleuth Chronicle from my backpack. I was just thirty dollars short from getting my own iPad, which I would use to digitize my detective business. The Sleuth Chronicle was almost full, and no self-respecting detective ran their business on paper these days.

Mine was the second-to-last stop, and the bus was almost full. It echoed with chatter and laughter and smelled like moldy oranges.

"Now through the weekend." March rolled his eyes

before facing the front of the bus. He was tall and skinny with crazy wide eyes. Somehow he had gotten the flat side of his hair to fluff up since I saw him earlier that morning.

I shrugged. "I'm grounded for a full week—we couldn't hang out anyway."

March turned to me again, his eyebrows pulling together. "You've got to stop being so nosy about the dognapping ring."

I tapped my pen on the open notebook. "Impossible! I'm meant to solve crime." Like studying for a test, detecting felt like the logical thing to do. Mom called that feeling *atarimae*. If you saw an old lady struggling to bring in her groceries, then you helped her bring in her groceries: atarimae. If you made a ginormous mess creating a papier-mâché weremonkey, you cleaned it all up—even the newspaper globs that somehow lodged beneath the tabletop, hardened like cement, and made your dad swear when he found them: atarimae.

And if dogs in your town were disappearing and you knew you could find the dognapper, you solved the crime and saved the day: atarimae.

I guessed that Mom felt the same way about curating exhibitions, and Dad felt the same way about engineering.

"You're a kid, Kazu. Kids don't solve crime."

"Willie Johnson was just twelve when he won the Medal of Honor during the Civil War," I said. "Joan of

11

Arc was thirteen when she led the French army to victory. And David was fourteen when he killed Goliath."

I opened my notebook. "The only thing holding us back from saving the planet is right up here." I tapped my temple with the pen. "And grown-ups—they're kind of a bummer, too."

He leaned into me, looking over my shoulder at the Sleuth Chronicle. It was an aquamarine leather-bound journal where I recorded all the objective facts, deductions, and clues on current cases. I flipped past the Fourth-Grade Lunch-Box Thief, the Raffle-Ticket Conspiracy, and the PE Teacher Shapeshifter Rumor to land on Denver Dognappings.

I stopped on a page labeled *Suspects*, wrote down Mrs. Fitzman's name, and then crossed her out, since she had been both suspected and cleared that same morning.

Also crossed out: Eugene the garbage collector, March's fourth-grade teacher, Mr. Hildebrandt, and the animal control lady who took Genki thirteen months ago when he jumped the fence to chase a couple of squirrels who had it out for him. He's a sucker for squirrels.

I snapped the notebook shut and wrapped it with a red rubber band from the paper route. Folded newspaper articles about Denver's Dognapping Ring were stuffed inside and ruffled beneath the band.

"I can't believe your mom's still letting you do the paper route by yourself."

"With Genki, she never cared before. But after this morning, she might start driving me again. And not to protect *us* from the dognapper, but to protect the neighborhood from *me*." Disappointing Mom seemed to be another of my natural reflexes.

March nodded, hugging a thick binder to his chest. I was sure all of his homework was neat and complete inside. "It's picture day today." He cocked his head, examining me. "Are you ready?"

I smoothed my hair with flat palms. In all the commotion of the morning, Mom must have forgotten. I looked at my jeans, the knees split wide, and my oversize gray T-shirt with a stain on the chest. "Um . . . My sentence may be longer than one week once this outfit is documented."

March shook his head and sighed. Then he held out his hand, an invitation to a thumb war, and we finger-wrestled the rest of the drive to school, March winning every time. That kid had freakishly strong thumbs.

Mrs. Hewitt bounced on her heels behind the music stand as she told us the story of *Oliver!*, her all-time favorite musical. The first song she wanted us to learn was called "Food, Glorious Food." Apparently, it was about a bunch of starving orphans who had a hankering for sausage-based dishes.

Mrs. Hewitt was suspiciously enthusiastic about this year's Thanksgiving concert, insisting we prepare early so that we could be Broadway-ready. She paced like a solider in front of the room, reciting the lyrics. But as she got more into it, she began to sing, her white hair bobbing to the beat. She belted out the ending, and some of the girls covered their ears as she shrieked, "FOOD, glorious food, glorious fooooooooooooood!"

Silence filled the room for a moment before cackling erupted from pockets in the choral risers. Madeleine Brown, the only other Asian girl in the fifth grade, led a group in giggling fits followed by whispering and then more giggling.

Madeleine was a whole head taller than me and her hair was long and wavy, while mine was straight, barely dipping below my shoulders. She was a soccer star who always wore athletic gear to school, including, sometimes, cleats. Today she had on a team hoodie and running capris. Even without spiked shoes, kids avoided her in the hallways; getting elbowed by Madeleine Brown could take you out for an entire recess.

While we had talked a bunch of times, all I really knew about Madeleine was that she was Korean and had been adopted as a baby. And she didn't like me. In fact, I was pretty sure she hated me.

In second grade her mom invited me to her princess unicorn birthday party because she wanted Madeleine to have an Asian friend. "I'll have to talk to your mom about more playdates," she had said, leading me into their bonus room, where all the girls twirled in tulle princess skirts made especially for the party.

Her mother left us to ourselves as we started to play. Everyone knelt around the birthday girl, seated on a golden metal folding chair, the taffeta from her Princess Celestia headband getting caught on the backrest. I had joined in, used to taking charge of imaginary games, and found myself calling out instructions to Madeleine Brown's guests. When I asked everyone to name a magical unicorn of their own, Madeleine took over and called on the girls one by one. I had started the game because I had the perfect unicorn name: Sunshine Lilly Buttercup, but when it was my turn, Madeleine skipped right over me.

One of the girls noticed and called out, "You forgot Kazu." Madeleine cut her eyes at the girl before turning toward me.

"She doesn't ride a magical unicorn," Madeleine snapped. "She has a donkey." The other girls laughed nervously.

"I do not," I had said as I slouched in my spot, concentrating on the sandy carpet strands so that I wouldn't cry. I stayed like that for the rest of the party, and Madeleine continued to ignore me.

When it was time to leave, Madeleine called after me, her voice sour and mean. "See you later, Bossy Jones."

On the risers, Madeleine stood above the group of sporty girls surrounding her. They all wore some combination of red and black: Lincoln Elementary School colors. As she leaned over to whisper into her neighbor's ear, she met my eyes and snapped straight up, like a skittish cat seeing a bulldog. I scrunched my eyebrows together, wondering what Madeleine Brown had to be afraid of.

The girls around her paused and then followed her gaze to where I stood in the middle of the first riser. Madeleine had a look like she was working out a story problem in her head. Then she took a deep breath, squared her shoulders, and called out, "Hey, Detective Jones! What are *you* looking at?" Kids around her snickered, and a prickly heat climbed my neck.

Most kids knew me as Detective Girl, and up through fourth grade everyone seemed to think it was cool that I liked unraveling mysteries. I carried the Sleuth Chronicle everywhere and asked probing questions when I thought someone might have information I needed for a case. But fifth grade was different from fourth grade. The same kids who thought it was cool last year were starting to roll their eyes at me this year. It all felt very shaky, like a towering Jenga bridge I had to cross. But no one had ever made fun of me about it out loud.

I searched for March and found him a couple rows above Madeleine Brown. He had heard, and his eyes were so wide I thought his eyeballs might plop from his head. I reached deep into my pockets and found the Jolly Rancher Ms. Packer had given us for quiet reading that day. With newspaper aim, I pulled my arm back and went to throw the candy at Madeleine Brown, whispering to myself, "Block this, soccer head!" as Mrs. Hewitt tapped her baton on the music stand, silencing the room. The sound distracted me, and I released the candy way too soon, launching it toward Mrs. Hewitt and hitting her on the cheek. As if on cue, the entire class gasped and turned to look at me.

Mrs. Hewitt pressed a hand to her cheek and spun toward my riser. "Ms. Jones?"

I opened my mouth to apologize, to explain, but it felt like my lungs were empty, and I had forgotten how to breathe.

Mrs. Hewitt scanned the room, her gaze landing on Madeleine, who was shaking with laughter. "I would like you and Ms. Brown to stay after school today. I have a special assignment for you both."

Madeleine pivoted to me again, her eyes blazing.

I smirked back and let myself enjoy the moment, because I knew that every second that followed was sure to be miserable.

CHAPTER THREE

Madeleine and I stood on opposite ends of the music room, our arms folded across our chests. Mrs. Hewitt swept through the doorway holding a bright yellow folder. She opened it and pulled out two sheets of paper—one for Madeleine and another one for me.

"What is *this*?" Madeleine held the sheet music away from her body like it was a banana peel.

Mrs. Hewitt sighed loudly. "I saw what happened in class today, ladies." She leveled us with a look. "And because I'm a music teacher, we're going to resolve *this*"— she gestured wildly at the space between Madeleine and me—"with song."

I raised my hand. "I'm really not much of a singer—"

Mrs. Hewitt cut me off. "It's a lovely song, and for two weeks I want you both to stay after school on Monday and practice this duet. If, by any chance, you don't cooperate and do your best, that two weeks will become three, which will become four and so forth."

I glared at the song's title, in all caps at the top of the page: "WE'RE GOING TO BE FRIENDS." This was a joke, right? I glanced around the room to see if maybe Ms. Smith, the principal, was hiding somewhere, ready to burst out laughing. Instead, I met Madeleine's eyes. We finally had something else in common—mortification.

"My mom—" Madeleine started, but Mrs. Hewitt interrupted.

"Your parents have been notified." She walked around the piano and bent over the keys. "Right now, they think you're participating in an extra-credit music assignment. I would be happy to call them back and explain that this activity has since devolved to detention."

The sharpness of her tone rang through the room. She was a tough cookie, Mrs. Hewitt. I wasn't going to test her. Besides, after what had happened that morning, I couldn't afford to get into any more trouble with Mom.

Without introduction, Mrs. Hewitt played the melody to "We're Going to Be Friends." After she'd finished, she waited a couple beats before saying, "Ready?"

Madeleine Brown and I stumbled our way through the first verse of the song.

I ran back to Mrs. Thomas's class to grab my backpack before Mom came to pick me up from school. All the kids had left the classroom except CindeeRae Lemmings, teacher's pet. Since school started, I had heard CindeeRae talk about her younger brother, soccer tryouts, her new Hot Stick rollers, all the books she was reading for the genre challenge, and of course, her lead as Annie, which had played at the Civic Auditorium that summer.

But unlike all the other times CindeeRae had come up to her desk to talk, Mrs. Thomas was not smiling with all her perfectly white teeth showing. Instead, Mrs. Thomas patted CindeeRae's back while she cried, big dollops that left a slick spot on her desk.

"We got Lobster for Christmas two years ago. We named him that because he has red hair, too. He's an Irish setter, and everyone loves him." I couldn't be sure, but it looked like a string of snot was hanging from CindeeRae's nose to the desktop. Mrs. Thomas must have noticed, too, because she pushed a handful of Kleenex toward her. CindeeRae cleaned herself up. "Who steals dogs? That's the meanest thing I've ever heard." Speaking that truth out loud must have made her even sadder, because she collapsed to the desk again, her shoulders bouncing with hiccuping sobs.

"Sweetie." Mrs. Thomas pushed a strand of red curly hair from CindeeRae's face and tucked it behind her ear. "Why don't we call your mom so she can give you a ride home?"

CindeeRae sat up, her shoulders still hunched, and wiped tears from her face with the backs of both hands. Her cheeks were all splotchy and her breath uneven. She caught me watching her but didn't look away. I thought of Genki and how sad I would be if he disappeared. I gave her a sad smile and she nodded at me like she understood.

"Okay, hon," Mrs. Thomas said, guiding CindeeRae into the hall with a hand on her shoulder. "You head to the office and call your mom for a ride home." We both watched her walk away, dragging her purple backpack behind her with one hand.

Mrs. Thomas turned around and smiled at me, all the shiny bangles on her wrists jingling as she brought her hands to her hips. "What are you still doing here, Kazu?"

"I stayed after for extra credit in music class." I lifted my backpack from its hook, not meeting Mrs. Thomas's eyes.

"Oh," she said. *"Extra credit."*

She drew the words out like something hid between the syllables. I realized she knew exactly what *extra credit* was code for.

"Don't forget your homework folder." She pulled it from my cubby and handed it to me.

I swung the backpack over my shoulder and clasped the gray folder to my chest. "Thanks, Mrs. Thomas. See you tomorrow."

As I waited for Mom by the big window in the office, I watched CindeeRae walk from the school to where her mom was parked at the curb. I couldn't be sure, but I thought it looked like her mom's eyes were red and swollen, too. The Denver Dognapping Ring had grown by one Lobster, and it really was the meanest thing ever.

CHAPTER FOUR

In addition to my paper route, I had two side jobs after school, because I was an enterprising individual. Mom would say that sounded braggy of me, but I was all about spreading truth, even if it made me look good.

One of my side jobs was walking the Tanners' Labradoodle on Mondays, Wednesdays, and Fridays. They lived next door, and Genki went berserk every time he saw me walk Barkley past our house. Today he jumped onto our bench seat and scratched at the window, his paws pedaling against the glass like he was working some doggie magic on us.

Barkley looked over her shoulder, kind of snobbish, and kept prancing.

We walked to the corner of Honeysuckle and down

Mom drove me around Lakeview Park and the surrounding neighborhoods so I could look for Barkley. The clouds seemed to darken and drop as we searched up and down the streets.

I called out my window weakly, almost certain that Barkley had been snatched and not lost. When she got scared she would roll onto her back and whimper, a little pee spotting the ground, and I wondered if the dognapper would yell at her for wetting the back of their van.

The radio was off, although Mom still tapped out a beat with her fingers on the steering wheel. She cleared her throat after I finished going over the whole story for what felt like the millionth time and said, "That doesn't seem like Barkley. Something must have caused her to pull away from you like that."

I picked at a spot on my jeans. "The blacksmith dropped his tools. I think it scared her." At least *that* part was true.

"That would do it," Mom said, turning back onto Honeysuckle. "Genki would have come back for you, though. He always comes back for you."

Genki would have made a better human than me. If I had taken him today he would have protected Barkley,

28

Morningside to Lakeview Park, which didn't have a lake so much as an overgrown pond with too much algae. This summer March and I spent three hours trying to free our Frisbee from beyond the tall grass where it had landed, in the mucky part we called the Swamp. We never got the Frisbee back, and for eight days March thought he had microcystin poisoning from the algae, which can make you puke, and blister on your lips. He only got a stomachache and a red bump on his palm from flicking a tree branch in and out of the water, but he still thought he was dying.

I took Barkley on the walkway that circled the entire park, past the soccer and baseball fields, two playlands, and a huge water fountain. When I got to the shady path behind the Pioneer Village and museum, I let Barkley off her leash to run ahead of me. The Tanners had never told me *not* to let Barkley off her leash, but they had never given me permission, either. She always got antsy toward the end, and this seemed to help. Plus, I had been walking her for six months now, and she had never once run away.

Until today.

As we passed the backside of Pioneer Village, a blacksmith stepped from his tiny log cabin, dropped his tools and they clanged together. The noise rang out like a gunshot, echoing between the old-timey buildings. Barkley jumped in surprise and shot down the shady path, her

25

tail waving behind her. I froze as I watched her flop off before I finally snapped out of it and chased after her. She turned toward the overflow parking lot for the museum and disappeared.

My legs ached as I ran to catch up, but the trees lining the path blocked my view, and I couldn't see which direction she went. Guessing left—the way we usually walked back home—I followed the road through the middle of the park and to the end of Summer Glen. Turning in circles, my eyes darting wildly around the park, I willed Barkley to jump back into my line of sight.

My heart rattled in my chest and my hands shook as I glimpsed a young boy walking his fluffy white dog toward Federal Boulevard and a young family cycling toward the playground. A soccer team practiced in the field, and two black Labs pulled at their leashes while the owner stood still, watching kids dribble a ball in and out of a long line of orange cones.

Barkley would have run to the dogs, hoping to play. Where was she?

I stared at no-Barkley until my vision blurred. Then I spun back toward the museum and retraced my steps to all her favorite pit stops: the garbage can by the baseball field, the base of the water fountain, the shelter by the playground.

As I rounded the corner of the shady path for the second time, a van screeched to a halt. I was in the middle of the road, my arms raised to block the blow, but it had just missed me. Dad complained about the speed limit in the park all the time, claiming turtles moved faster than twelve miles per hour. But this van was going way faster than that, and it seemed weird anyone would be in that much of a hurry leaving Pioneer Village. I panted, trying to catch my breath, and realized that if I wanted to, I could reach out and write my name in the dirt caked on the van's hood.

I was waiting for the angry driver to step out and lecture me, frozen like a criminal with my hands up, wh[en] I heard a yip. Muffled maybe, but I could have swor[n] was Barkley crying in the back of the van. It revved [h] and screeched again, only this time it sped around and out Lakeview Park.

Barkley's leash hung empty from my hand, [I] was walking a ghost dog. Had that van taken her [?] I closed my eyes and tried to remember what it l[ooked] like, but all I could picture was my name written [in] dirty hood.

I stood in front of a garbage can and twis[ted] leash around my hand, watching my fingertips t[urn] I couldn't tell the Tanners I broke the leash la[tch] Barkley run straight into a dognapping ring. I [f] let Barkley loose, she wouldn't have been sw[ept] leash proved my guilt. I untangled the pink lea[sh] grip, tossed it into the trash, and raced home.

because he always came through in a pinch. I didn't even recognize him when he thought someone in our family was being threatened. Jimmy Mason had chased me home from the bus stop one day in third grade and Genki jumped the fence and circled him like a frothing were-monster, while I had watched all curious to see if Genki was going to kill him or not. Later, Mom had yelled at me for not calling Genki off, but I knew my hesitation meant Jimmy Mason would never bother me again. And so far he hadn't.

"It's not Barkley's fault," I said. "It's my fault, and the Tanners are going to hate me forever." *That* part was true, too.

Mom slowed as we neared home. "You need to tell them." She pulled ahead to the Tanners' house next door. "Do you want me to come with you?"

"No." Mom had already heard me lie once today; I didn't want to double-up on all that dishonesty. "I'll go alone."

I walked to the Tanners' front door, my heart knocking around my chest like a caged bird. Hearing our car hum behind me, I turned around and waved Mom away. She put the car in reverse and slowly backed toward our house and into the driveway. She didn't get out.

Taking a big breath, I knocked on the door. Mrs. Tanner answered, breathless, her big baby belly peeking past the door frame. She smiled, but when her gaze dropped to my side and found nothing, she looked back at me, her eyes a little wild. "Where's Barkley?"

"I'm so sorry," I said, tears holding to my lashes. "The blacksmith scared her on the shady path and she ran away."

Mrs. Tanner's hand rose to her mouth and stayed there. She had once told me that she and her husband had gotten Barkley as newlyweds in college. Barkley was their practice baby, she had joked; they were preparing for the real deal sometime around Thanksgiving.

"Mom and I drove all around the park," I said. "And through all the Lakeview neighborhoods. We still couldn't find her." The tears paused at my chin and then slid down my neck.

Mrs. Tanner's eyes had filled with tears, too. She finally broke from her trance. For a second it looked like she was going to bend over to my level, but then she put her hand on my shoulder instead. "It's not your fault, sweetie. Barkley's easily spooked."

We both stood there, not looking at each other. The tulips in the flower beds had lost all their petals, and the stalks stood tall and naked. I didn't know what you do after telling someone you lost their practice baby.

"I'm sorry for crying, Kazuko. It's all these pregnancy hormones. I'm sure we'll find Barkley in no time." Her voice got chokey. "I'll call Frank right now so he can come home early and start looking."

I nodded and asked if she wanted me to help them hang flyers. With all the dogs that had gone missing, there wasn't a lamppost or telephone pole that didn't have a missing dog flyer stapled to it.

"It's sweet of you to ask. I'll let you know." The tears were rolling down her cheeks now, and she shut the door just as her face broke into the ugly cry.

I stood there for a moment, listening to her sobs fade as she moved away from the door.

CHAPTER FIVE

I cleared a spot in the middle of my bedroom and spread my free newspaper on the floor like wrapping paper. Genki nosed at me while I tried to concentrate, so I scrunched his face between my hands, rubbed his nose with mine, and said, "How's my puppy?" After a good scratching behind the ears, he lay next to me, stretching out so that his side nuzzled my leg.

My fingers, still black with ink from the route, shook a little as I smoothed out the front page. The headline read DENVER'S DOGNAPPING RING EMBOLDENED: THREE DOGS REPORTED MISSING IN ONE DAY. Three pictures hung beneath the headline and above the fold. Barkley was in the middle, looking royal as she sat at attention.

On the far right, CindeeRae Lemmings's dog, Lobster, lay in the grass.

The words blurred on the page. The thought of Barkley bounding out of sight swelled in my mind, taking up all the space. I stood and searched my room for the Sleuth Chronicle, knocking down book towers and scattering clothing piles as I scrambled to find my notebook. Genki followed me, sniffing each place I searched.

The corner of my notebook peeked from beneath the bed, and I snatched it up and returned to the newspaper. Genki sat for a second, cocking his head to the side as if trying to decide whether he wanted to risk cozying up to me again. Instead, he jumped on my bed and pawed at my covers, making a doggie nest.

I scratched down important facts:

- One of the dogs was grabbed from its yard at night, and two were taken during the day.
- And of the two, only one was on a leash: Barkley.

Only that was a lie, because I couldn't stand to tell the Tanners it was my fault Barkley went missing. Mr. Tanner had come over the night before to ask more questions before reporting Barkley as a missing dog. I told him she had pulled loose, yanking the leash from my hands because the blacksmith had startled her. There had to be some curse I would experience for telling the same lie three times in one day.

The article went on to say there were no leads, except for the one I hadn't shared: A dirty van was taking the dogs away. I wrote that piece of information upside down and backward in case someone snooped through my notebook.

Last week the police had shut down an illegal puppy mill on the outskirts of town where four dogs that had disappeared over the summer were found; they had been used as breeders, caged inside an abandoned apartment complex with dozens of other dogs, some of them mal-nourished. All of them dirty and sad. The National Mill Dog Rescue had taken sixty-three puppies to distribute to no-kill shelters across the state. Apparently illegal puppy mills like tiny dogs because they can cram more of them into tight spaces: Chihuahuas, Yorkies, terriers, miniature poodles, and pinschers. While some of the missing dogs were being sold to puppy mills, others, they suspected, were going to breeders, dogfighting rings, or laboratories conducting scientific experiments.

I tried shrugging off the chills that rounded my back, but they lingered at my shoulder blades. Where would Barkley go?

A darkness settled in my stomach like a stone.

I ripped the front page from the paper, folded it care-fully, and stuck it in the pages of my Sleuth Chronicle.

From downstairs, I could hear Mom call, "Kazuko!"

My name was Japanese and meant child of harmony. Mom was second-generation Japanese, which meant that while her parents were born in Japan, she was born in America. Raised in Seattle by my Ba-chan and Ji-chan, she could speak Japanese but felt more comfortable with English. My grandparents named her Yumi, but by the time she was in second grade, she was going by Rachel. After I was born, Mom became a born-again Nihonjin for a few years, and I learned what little Japanese I knew then. But now, aside from eating the occasional traditional dish and repeating a few phrases I knew, I wasn't much of a cultural expert.

Hearing Mom, Genki sat up and wagged his tail. My alarm clock read 7:55. The bus would come in ten minutes. I changed clothes, pulling them from a crumpled pile on my floor, and then dashed down the stairs.

"Hustle!" Mom yelled, watching me from the front door. "You're going to miss the bus."

I slipped my shoes on. Mom's mouth gaped when she noticed the holes in the knees of my jeans—the same ones I had worn yesterday.

"Kazuko Jones!" she snapped. "School started two weeks ago. You have plenty of new clothes to wear before resorting to old holey jeans."

I picked at the hem of my shirt. "Aren't you glad your daughter isn't worried about phony things like name brands and unholey jeans?" I met her eyes. "I'm a humble person, Mom."

"If you have to tell someone you're humble, chances are you're really not. But nice try."

She stepped back to look at me, clicking her tongue and shaking her head. I knew the dilemma: Her daughter was late and wearing damaged clothing. She could make me change, but then I'd miss the bus and she would have to drive me to school, and getting driven to school didn't build character.

She shooed me out the door while blocking Genki from following me and waved good-bye.

That morning at school we had a safety assembly first thing. As my class walked to the auditorium I heard muffled conversations about kidnapper clowns, twisty hair tutorials, and missing dogs.

I watched as CindeeRae walked into the auditorium ahead of me, her head bowed so low that her red ringlets hid her face like a veil. Before Lobster disappeared, CindeeRae had been the chattiest person in the fifth grade with the least friends. Maybe it was because she wouldn't let anyone forget about her lead performance in *Annie*, which I guessed she'd probably won more with her hair than her acting. But now that CindeeRae's dog had vanished, I felt bad for giving her the stink-eye every time she gushed about the theater.

The room echoed with laughter as students elbowed past one another, jockeying for seats next to friends while Mrs. Thomas and the reading aide guided them with loopy gestures. Ahead of me Sky Mendelson and Finn Clayson shot spitballs from red straws, hitting friends rows ahead before turning on each other. I kept my distance, wondering if Lobster had met Barkley yet, and if they could be friends, wherever they were sent.

Principal Smith stood at the front of the room, folding her arms like a proper example of respectable behavior. One policeman stood on the stage, his arms stiff at his sides. I searched for March in the class behind mine and found him looking wildly about the room. When he saw me, he smiled wide before flashing our secret hand signal—*Taco Monster* in sign language. I returned the gesture, making a hard taco shell with one hand and filling it with the fingers of the other before bringing both hands up in monster claws. Then I sat down, squaring my notebook on my lap and looking straight ahead.

Mr. Grobin, the school counselor, walked onto the middle of the stage in front of the microphone stand. He was tall and thin, and everything about him was ironed and tucked in. His white hair stuck to his scalp like a swim cap.

"Good morning, students," he said.

A handful of kids greeted him in return. "Good morning."

He stood quietly until the room settled.

"We're here to talk about safety."

Mr. Grobin waited again as students leaned into their neighbors, whispering. He rubbed his hands together like they were cold. "We want you to know that your well-being is our first priority. I'm sure you've heard that some beloved local pets have gone missing, some of them pets of your own." Down the aisle, CindeeRae bent over her knees like she needed to hurl. And sure enough, with a disgusting retching sound, she did.

Mrs. Thomas shuffled toward her from the side of the auditorium while Sky and Carl made barf faces at each other. The smell of puke floated out like a green fog, and I covered my nose to stop my stomach from heaving. As the boys clutched their guts and rolled in their chairs, Mrs. Thomas ushered CindeeRae from the room, and even from behind I could tell she was crying again. Custodian Clark appeared like a magician, covering the mess with sawdust and disappearing before the sweet smell of cleaner could mix with the urpy smell of CindeeRae's sadness.

While the stench spread across the auditorium almost as quickly as the story, Mr. Grobin tapped the microphone and said, "Listen up."

When the chatting continued, he yelled, "Settle

down," and around me students hushed and turned to the front.

The room quieted, except for the noise of kids shifting in their seats.

Mr. Grobin basked in the silence for a few seconds. "We want to remind you of some safety rules. This is Officer Maxwell, and he's going to instruct you how to respond in the event you see a dognapping."

Mr. Grobin stepped back and gestured to Officer Maxwell, who took the microphone off its stand and paced the stage. He talked about being extra-observant and not getting involved if we witnessed a dognapping, because we didn't know how dangerous these people might be.

I leaned back and looked at the ceiling, taking deep breaths and counting slowly in my mind. I saw Barkley launch ahead of me on the shady path and disappear. It was my fault she was missing. And it was my responsibility to save her.

Suddenly, the image in my mind darkened, and it wasn't Barkley but Genki disappearing into the dirty van at six in the morning, the wheels on my baby-blue Schwinn cruiser spinning, and unbound newspapers fanning out in the street as I chased after it. My head snapped up. My heart was beating so fast, I was certain my neighbors could hear it, and when I turned to check, my pulse echoed in my ears.

The Sleuth Chronicle fell from my lap with a thud.

CHAPTER SIX

My parents talked about Mom's new exhibit for the museum while we ate dinner. The Perception Center was a long-term interactive display that had been at the Denver Exploration Museum for Kids three years now, and it was Mom's job to design something to replace it. Something sensational.

"What do you think about a baking center?" she asked me and Dad. "Hands-on with measuring cups and lessons on fractions." Mom brainstormed ideas aloud. "Play markets are big these days, or maybe a water study with one of those gigantic bubble rings you can stand inside of?"

"That last one sounds promising." Dad placed his

chopsticks across the middle of his bowl of udon, still full of the thick noodles swimming in dark broth. He looked at me for a response, and I shrugged. Mom was just getting started and needed to burn through the boring ideas before she got to the good stuff.

"Why so quiet, Bug?" he asked.

"I'm not."

My parents exchanged looks, and I knew they were thinking about Barkley.

"Can we have pizza casserole for dinner tomorrow night?" Talking about dinner seemed safer than talking about missing pets. I needled the bowl with my chopsticks, trying to avoid the blob of nattō nesting in the middle of my noodles.

"We don't eat Japanese food *that* often," Mom said. "Besides, this is a perfectly healthy dinner, with less preservatives."

"But nattō smells funny." Nattō was fermented soybeans that were probably healthy because all the toxins in your body evacuated as soon as you ate it.

"It's an acquired taste. Plus, it's good for you," Mom said.

I sat back in my seat and pushed my hands into my pockets, not even pretending to eat. Deep in the corner on the left side was the sheet music for "We're Going to Be Friends," crumpled and frayed. I pulled it out and smoothed the edges on the tabletop.

41

Mom studied the paper and smiled. "Is that your extra credit for music class?"

Before I could answer, Dad snatched the paper and began to sing the words, his deep baritone voice rumbling across the table and making Genki howl from where he lay beneath my chair.

"I have to sing it with Madeleine Brown," I said.

"The unicorn princess?" Mom asked. Back in those days I told Mom everything, and she still remembered all of it. Now I mostly shared stuff with March, even though Mom displayed sharp detecting abilities in the questions she drilled me with every day after school. Evading her questions required as much skill as asking them, I had discovered.

"Yes." I used my chopsticks to pick up the napkin next to my bowl and dab my cheeks with it. "She's still as mean as ever. Only now with soccer cleats."

"Well," Dad said, "this is one of my favorite White Stripes songs. I expect a solo performance once your extra credit is complete."

I didn't answer and continued to poke at my noodles with the chopsticks.

"Kazu?" Mom leaned over to trap my gaze. "Are you still upset about Barkley?"

I set my chopsticks on the edge of my bowl. "The Tanners think I'm the worst."

"They're just upset Barkley's gone," Dad said. "That's not your fault, Bug."

I thought of Barkley's leash in the garbage can next to the museum parking lot. It *was* my fault. "I would hate me if I lost Genki."

"No one's losing Genki," Mom said.

Hearing his name, Genki startled from under the table, knocking his head on the crossbeam of my chair. I swung my leg until I found his belly and rubbed at him with my foot. "CindeeRae from my class lost her dog, too. His name is Lobster, and they took him from her backyard in the middle of the night."

Mom reached over and put her hand on mine. "They'll catch the dognapper, Kazu."

She was being too gushy, and I fidgeted in my seat. Mom grabbed Mrs. Hewitt's sheet music and folded it, her fingers flying like she was casting a spell. She dropped it back in its place, only this time it was a dog with triangle ears and a tail that curved around its body like a question mark. It looked a little like Barkley.

"Do you think I'm a weirdo?" I asked as I cradled the dog in my palm.

Dad chuckled. "Aren't we all?"

Detective Mom set her chopsticks down and studied me. "What makes you ask?"

"Sometimes kids make fun of my investigations."

"Kazuko Jones," Dad said, leaning over his elbows and showing horrible table manners. "I expect you to be a spectacular weirdo."

Mom and I both looked at him, waiting for the punch line.

"Ordinary is boring," he explained. "If you didn't stand out for something, I would worry about you."

"But," Mom interrupted, "balance is important, too. You've become a little too obsessed with this detective business, and it's getting you into trouble."

Gah! Why couldn't adults just answer a simple question without getting so preachy? "I know," I said, because it meant I understood, but it didn't mean I agreed.

"I, for one," Dad said, "will stand out amongst my family by eating this nattō in one bite."

"Carl!" Mom scowled as Dad pinched the giant dollop of nattō with his chopsticks and dropped it into his mouth.

I scrunched my nose.

Dad winked at Mom before turning back to me, talking with his mouth full. "Nattō is great!" Bits of beans clung to the top of his tongue.

"Stop talking with your mouth full," Mom said. When Dad swallowed and showed her his clean tongue, she added, "You're disgusting."

He leaned over and kissed her right on the mouth.

"See?" Dad said. "Nattō level, unlocked."

I said, "Now I've definitely lost my appetite. Can I be excused?" Usually I couldn't leave the table until my dinner was gone, and I'd hardly eaten three full bites of the udon and none of the nattō.

"I guess," Mom said. "But do you mind if I tag along on the route tomorrow? It's starting to get chilly out."

Since I was nine years old I had done the paper route by myself from spring until late fall, when it either snowed or the temperature dropped below zero. Then, because death was a possibility, Mom drove me. But with Barkley becoming Denver's seventeenth missing dog, she may have started to see Genki as dognapping bait.

Dad reached over and squeezed Mom's hand.

"I guess," I answered, trying to hide my relief at her offer. Balancing my bowl in one hand and Origami Barkley in the other, I pushed away from the table and left the room. Genki, triggered by the sound of my chair scraping the floor, emerged from under the table and followed me.

"Kazuko! Wake up!" Mom yelled from the bottom of the stairs.

"Coming!" I rolled onto the floor and patted around

me for the pink jacket I set out every night before going to sleep. Genki unwound from his spot at the foot of my bed and nosed my face like he did every morning. I couldn't tell if he was upset I had woken him up or anxious to get to work.

"I love you too, pup pup." I held his ears and pressed my forehead against his. He pushed his nose into my ear, sniffing like he'd found treasure. "Okay, okay. Let's go."

My room was dark and cold, and the numbers on my clock flashed 12:00. That usually meant the electricity had gone out sometime in the middle of the night, which explained why my alarm hadn't gone off.

"Hurry, Kazuko!" Mom banged her hand on the wall.

"Sheesh," I muttered under my breath.

I pulled on my jacket and trudged down the stairs, Genki tumbling down ahead of me. Mom waited by the door in her nightshirt, her robe pulled tight at her waist. I was still in my PJs, too. No one dressed up for the paper route.

I slid my shoes on and followed Mom out the door to our driveway, where a bundle of newspapers sat by the curb. Genki trotted behind me as I carried the bundle to the car and set it on the console, ripping off the yellow plastic strap that held them together. While Mom started the car, I rolled papers with rubber bands and lined them on the dash. I punched the cab light so I could still work while Mom drove.

Mom turned the radio on low, some nineties station that always played her favorite band, Smashing Pumpkins. She began the figure-eight loop that we followed to cover the three different streets on my route, her fingers playing the steering wheel like a piano even though the song was all about electric guitars. Genki paced in the backseat as she drove.

"All right, all right," Mom hollered at Genki in the backseat as she slowed for the first house. "I'll roll down the windows, but no chasing squirrels."

Genki was crazy for squirrels, so Mom could only roll the windows down halfway. "Ew," she said, watching him through the rearview. "I forget how slobbery he gets on car rides."

It had been months since Mom had driven me, so I had to remind her which houses got the newspaper. She would pull up in front of each, and I would run through front lawns, tossing papers onto doorsteps. People liked it when they could reach the paper without stepping outside; I think that's why I got such good tips at Christmas.

I tried to act natural as we rounded the corner of Morningside onto Colonial Avenue, passing Eleanor Fitzman's house on the corner. Mom rolled to a stop in front of March's house, which glowed white in the moonlight even though I knew it was really yellow.

I tossed a paper at March's porch and accidentally hit the door. In the quiet morning, the paper banged against their screen like a baseball. I half-expected March's bedroom light to turn on, but the house remained dark and silent.

Mom pulled up to the creepy house at the end of the street where I thought I had seen someone peer at us through the blinds yesterday morning. I stood in the middle of the walkway, ready to toss a paper to the porch without getting too close. But then I noticed a bag hung over the door handle, and I knew I'd have to grab it.

The first Monday each September, Mom printed off a note that I stuffed in every newspaper, thanking customers for leaving their porch lights on and recycling newspaper bags. We only used the bags when it rained or snowed, but they were expensive, and I paid for them out of my newspaper money. So every now and then someone hung a bag full of recycled newspaper bags from their door handle, and I took them home.

I tiptoed toward the door. If there's one thing I'd learned from my paper route, it was the older the customer, the earlier they woke up in the morning. This guy was a geezer and might open the door as I grabbed the bag, like the chain saw dude at a spook alley. My fingers brushed the doorknob as Mom rolled down the window. "Kazuko," she barked. "Hurry."

I jumped—squeaking a bit—then grabbed the bag and ran back to the car.

"My, aren't we jumpy," she said as I climbed into the front seat.

"You scared me, Mom. Don't do that."

She smiled and then changed her mind. *Barkley.* I knew that's what she was thinking as the smile faded from her face.

While Mom made breakfast I sorted the newspaper bags in the garage. Genki dragged the ratty garage blanket from behind Dad's tool cabinet and began kneading it into a nest.

There were two sizes of newspaper bags: yellow for the fat Sunday papers, and orange for the dailies. Geezer had stuffed probably a year's worth of newspaper bags into a Walmart sack. Two hampers sat in the corner of our garage packed with recycled newspaper bags, and as I pulled the bags out, one by one, I placed them in their designated baskets.

Genki stretched and tugged at the blanket to get his nest just right.

"We're not going to be here very long," I told him. He'd get comfortable about the same time I was ready to go back inside. Without looking at me, Genki pawed at the fabric, turning a slow circle around his shabby mound.

I separated the recycled bags into the two bins. Some people twisted each bag into a knot, thinking somehow that might help me. Those were the worst because they took longer to untangle. Others smoothed each bag out and then stacked them on top of one another so they looked like the sleeves newspaper bags came in. While these people had far too much time on their hands, they were my favorite because that made reusing the bags easier. Others stuffed them into a sack without any pattern or purpose. Geezer was *that* type of person, which was better than the knotters, but not quite as good as the smoothers.

Genki, satisfied with his blanket nest, circled it once more before plopping down.

I pulled out a fistful of bags as Mom opened the garage door from the kitchen. "Breakfast is ready."

"Just a minute."

"This morning I made your favorite." The smell of bacon wafted by, and she waved me in. Genki lifted his nose in the air, catching the smell, and then hopped up and trotted into the house.

"Traitor," I grumbled.

I wished parents realized that being extra nice made kids nervous. Mom and Dad worried about missing Barkley, and worried that I worried about missing Barkley. And believe me, I worried. But making bacon and Belgian waffles for breakfast made me feel worse about it all, like when Mom made a cake after my gerbil, Snickers, died. It felt like celebrating bad fortune, and that only seemed to invite more of it.

I dropped the handful of yellow bags into the hamper, reaching in to pull out a stray orange bag. In the bottom was a piece of paper—it looked like a receipt. I fished my hand into the bottom of the bag and pulled it out. It *was* a receipt, folded in half. I opened it.

"Kazu!" Mom had opened the garage door wide, and Genki stood behind her. I realized I had scrunched the receipt in a fist behind my back. "You still have to get dressed after you eat. Come inside." She slammed the door behind her.

I opened my hand. In the center of my palm lay the now-crumpled piece of paper. I smoothed it out again, the print facing me, and saw that Geezer had purchased just one thing: dog food. Fifteen bags of it.

And he didn't even have a dog.

CHAPTER SEVEN

I sat down on the bus next to March and handed him my route list and map while pulling the receipt from the Sleuth Chronicle.

"What's going on?" He closed the comic book he had been reading.

"This." I took back the papers, handed him the receipt, and pointed to the print beneath the King Soopers logo. "I found it inside a recycled newspaper bag this morning." My hands still shook.

Our bus driver followed the same figure-eight loop Mom and I had this morning, only backward. The bus driver picked up March at the top of the loop before backtracking down Morningside and then up Summer Glen. As we passed Geezer's house on Colonial, I pointed. "The recycled newspaper bag came from *that* house."

He studied the house, on his side of bus, and exhaled. "So?"

"So? That house doesn't even have a dog. We need to figure out who lives there."

I studied the map Dad had made when I first started the route. It was a perfect miniature of our neighborhood, tucked into the corner where Lakeview Park met Federal Boulevard. The streets in our area created a grid surrounding the park with houses that had once been some of the first and fanciest in town. Now most of the houses looked run-down and had a lot of old people living in them. March's house and my house were two of the few in our area with kids.

"March?"

He stared at the receipt. "This doesn't mean anything. Maybe he donated all that food to the animal shelter."

"Really? What kind of crazy person does that?" I went back to studying my map.

"I told you, Kazu," March said. "You've got to stop being so nosy about the dognappings."

We hadn't talked about the case since I detected Mr. Mapples's burial two days ago. A lot had happened since then. A lot that I hadn't told March.

I sat up straight and looked ahead, blowing out a long

breath. "I have to tell you something, and you can't tell anyone else."

March nodded.

"You know how I always let Barkley off her leash on the shady path?"

March nodded again.

"She ran away the last time I walked her. And while I was looking for her, I almost got run over by a dognapping van."

March's eyebrows nearly touched. "Barkley's gone?"

"Yes," I said, looking back at my map. "And it's *my* fault."

"Did you tell your mom?"

"That she was dognapped after I let her off her leash?" I turned to him. "Are you kidding?"

"If you saw the dognapper, you have to tell her."

"I don't have enough evidence to tell anyone anything yet. And do you remember how much trouble I'm in for reporting an old lady who was burying her pug? I'm already banned from calling the police unless someone is bleeding and/or not breathing."

March tapped his foot as I went back to studying the map. I said, "Can you imagine what my parents would say if I told them I think Mr. Geezer is the Denver Dognapper?"

"Whoa, whoa, whoa." March pushed the receipt back

at me, and I slid it back into the Sleuth Chronicle. "You don't know that he's the person responsible for all those missing dogs."

"Exactly! That's why we have to do some detective work." My finger found March's house on the map and moved down five tiny squares to Geezer's house: 2736 Colonial. I flipped the sheet over to find the address on my route list.

"That's Mr. Crowley's house," March said as my finger found the listing: James Crowley. "My parents send us over every year with a plate of Christmas cookies. He's old and creepy, but he's not a criminal."

"How do you know that?"

The bus stopped in front of Lincoln, and all the kids began shuffling down the aisle. I opened the Sleuth Chronicle to my Suspects page and wrote *James Crowley* beneath crossed-out *Mrs. Fitzman.*

"His wife died two years ago, of cancer or something. He's probably sadder than he is creepy. He keeps to himself—we only see him a couple times a year. My mom calls him a hobbit, but I think she really means hermit."

"And he loves dogs?"

March shook his head. "Mr. Crowley hates Hopper. When I was seven he yelled at me for letting him pee in his yard. He was so mad I thought the vein in his forehead would explode." Hopper was the Winterses' dog, a knee-high, rusty-colored mutt.

"See?"

"That doesn't mean he's a dognapper," March said. "Plus, if he hates dogs so much, he wouldn't go around stealing everyone else's."

March had a point. But the receipt! That was evidence, and we couldn't ignore evidence.

I slammed my notebook shut and stuffed it in my open backpack along with the map and route list.

"Okay. If you don't think he did it, you won't mind if we do a little spying. Just to make sure." The bus driver waved us out and we slowly made our way down the aisle.

"When you say 'spy,' I feel like I'm already grounded."

"You *are* already grounded." I looked at him over my shoulder. "Me too. But we can still work the case."

"I don't think that's such a good idea."

"Don't be such a guppy, Flounder," I said, because every time March acted like a scaredy-cat, I called him Flounder. He was silent all the way into the school and up to the spot at the top of the stairs where we parted ways to go to our different classrooms.

I knew March Winters. He may have been mad at me, but he would come around by the time I had named our operation and assigned him the job of Director of Computer Hacking. He would be unable to resist his life calling as boy genius of all things tech.

Besides. How could he refuse? We had a crime to solve.

I grabbed my chocolate milk and took my lunch where CindeeRae sat with a handful of kids from Mrs. Thomas's class. She picked at the lettuce and tomato slice from her hamburger, which sat open and dry on her tray.

"That looks gross," I said, sitting down across from her and waving March over from where we usually sat at the C table.

"Gee, thanks." She kept her eyes down while she talked.

"What I meant was, I can share mine if you want." I turned my paper bag upside down, each item that dropped to the tabletop making my face burn more.

When Mom had time, she packed a fancy lunch with a grilled ham and cheese tortilla, apple slices with caramel dipping sauce, and Chex Mix, all covered by a napkin with a gushy love note. But most days, when she scrambled to get me out the door so that she could get to work herself, she packed a quick-and-dirty lunch, like today.

The two slices of bread, smooshed by the jelly and peanut butter packets she had dropped into a sandwich bag, toppled to the table first, followed by a cracked hard-boiled egg. A bag full of celery sticks tumbled atop a small packet of Oreo cookies, and an apple rolled from the table onto the floor.

"Sorry." I blew out an apologetic breath. "Mine's grosser, I guess."

CindeeRae looked up and gave me a crooked smile. "It's not *that* bad," she said.

I pushed the Oreos to her. "Halfsies?"

She tentatively opened the package and took two, pushing the rest back to me. We smiled at each other as we ate.

March sat down next to me with Jared Cramer, his buddy from Mr. Carter's class. Pat, our friend from second grade, had followed them over and sat down next to CindeeRae.

"Hey, CindeeRae," March said as he unloaded his bag, which had some reddish dish in a Tupperware container that he would need to microwave. He swiped my hard-boiled egg and replaced it with a granola bar. He was following lunchtime exchange rules: Everything in the middle of the table was fair game as long as you replaced it with something from your own lunch.

"That wasn't up for trade." I pushed the granola bar toward him. "I was just looking through my lunch." Eyeing his offering, I changed my mind and pulled the granola bar and the rest of my lunch back.

Everyone made their own exchanges, which left a bag of carrot sticks, a packet of Fig Newtons, and a banana in the middle of the table. As everyone began eating, Pat got to work pretending to drink his milk through a straw stuck up his nose, alternating gulping noises with choking noises. By the time he got to the knock-knock jokes, CindeeRae was laughing just as hard as the rest of us.

Jared interrupted, whispering, "Guys, guys." His eyes swung toward the end of the cafeteria. "Look. Here comes Madeleine Brown."

She had stood up from the A table with her best friend, Catelyn Monsen, walking toward the exit. She wore baggy athletic shorts and a long-sleeved Under Armour shirt with a zip-up collar and holes in the wristbands for her thumbs.

"So?" March said.

"She's just scary." Jared shuddered as she neared, still speaking under his breath. "You need more than a Jolly Rancher to take *her* out."

Jared was in our music class and wouldn't let me forget what I had done to earn my extra-credit assignment from Mrs. Hewitt.

"Very funny," I said, just as Madeleine caught us watching her. She studied our group, that same thoughtful look on her face from before, and we all looked away, suddenly enthralled with our lunches.

Madeleine passed us but doubled back at the last minute. "What are you weirdos looking at?" She leaned over the table, her eyebrows high. Catelyn stood next to her, studying the ceiling like she was bored. I tried to imagine Madeleine singing our detention song to Catelyn and couldn't picture it. Did mean people have any real friends?

Everyone at our table watched Madeleine, silently. She unrumpled her own lunch sack and dumped all the garbage from inside onto our table. PB&J crusts, a half-empty Jell-O cup, and orange peels scattered atop our lunch trade.

"There, more junk for you to exchange," she said, dropping the sack dramatically on top of the mess she had made before walking away. Over her shoulder she called "You're welcome" in a singsong voice while Catelyn laughed so hard she snorted.

We looked at the garbage from Madeleine's lunch before braving glances at each other. The first one to break the silence was CindeeRae. "She's the worst!"

"Told you," Jared said.

Pat pretended to sneeze into his napkin, then showed everyone a splatter of mustard inside the folds. "Oh, look," he said. "I Madeleined all over the place."

I laughed with everyone else, even though Madeleine Brown's garbage piled atop our lunch trade made me feel small. My eyes stung and my stomach burned as I watched her leave the cafeteria. I swung from the bench, grabbed my apple from the floor, and threw it across the room, where it dropped into the garbage can as Madeleine Brown walked out the door.

"Great shot," March said.

"I missed."

I slumped back into my seat and finished my lunch.

CHAPTER EIGHT

Four afternoons in a row I showed up on March's porch, a thick manila folder hidden behind my back. And every time March answered the door, he gave me some lame excuse about having too much homework to hang out. Today *had* to be different.

"You've gotta help me," I said as soon as the door opened. Only instead of March standing in the open doorway, it was Maggie, his oldest sister and a senior at Lakeview High School.

"Sheesh, Kazu." She laughed. "All you had to do was ask."

"Sorry. I thought you were March."

Maggie was the prettiest Winters girl. She had dark, thick curls and ice-blue eyes, while March's—and the rest of his siblings'—were brown. She wore thick glasses that made her look super smart. College scouts were begging her to attend their fancy-pants schools when she graduated. She and March were most alike, and she had taught him everything he knew about computer programming—and, as long as his parents weren't listening, hacking. March would definitely go to a fancy-pants college when he graduated, too.

"Come in," she said, sweeping her arm out like a game-show model.

I walked into the house, nearly tripping over a pile of shoes in the entryway as Maggie moved toward the stairs. The layout of the Winterses' house was nearly identical to ours, but the atmosphere was completely different. Theirs was artsy and laid-back and a little sloppy, whereas ours was always super neat. Abstract paintings hung from the walls of the living room, except over the mantel, where pictures of the seven Winters kids were crammed. While the walls looked like an art gallery, the floor looked like a daycare center, with stacks of puzzles, games, clothing, blankets, and abandoned art projects scattered throughout the house. But even though it was cluttered, I was always drawn into the happy, warm mess of the Winters family. In my opinion, clutter was cozier than clean. But I would never say that in front of Mom.

"March!" Maggie yelled, her voice dropping a couple octaves and rumbling from somewhere deep in her throat. March had once called it her Satan voice, which seemed about right.

Music blared from behind someone's door upstairs— not March's, because he was tidy about everything, including noise.

Maggie shrugged when there was no response. "Go on up," she said. "Knock first. You never know when March will decide to study in his underwear."

We both laughed. March wore long pants all the time, even in the summer. He thought he was too thin. Even when Dad's boss invited us out on his boat, he would wear mesh gym pants and a tank top. Every. Single. Time.

I made my way up the stairs, stepping around an avalanche of Matchbox cars, probably belonging to Mason, Miles, and Max, March's younger brothers. Sure enough, the boys were crowded into the room at the end of the hall, building an intricate track that dropped from the top bunk down the length of the bottom bunk before sloping to the floor, where it wound around the room.

"Hey, guys," I said.

"Hi, Kazu." Mason was the only one who looked up from their work as I knocked on March's door. Mason was nine and shared a room with March, but he rarely spent any time there on account of March nagging him to clean up before he could even think about making a mess. So Mason mostly hung out with Miles and Max, who were seven and five, creating crazy messes around the house that March couldn't say boo about.

"Come in!"

I opened March's door. I had always thought that his bedroom belonged in my house, and my bedroom belonged in his. March's room was neat like a hotel room with clean dresser tops and vacuumed corners. Galaxy bedspreads hung over each bunk with precision, as if March had used a ruler to calculate overhang. He sat at his desk, looked over his shoulder when I walked in, and quickly turned back to his computer, where he was working on something brainy.

While the tidiness of it all made my head hurt, I loved the walls, painted a deep purple and spotted with tiny glow-in-the-dark stars. Strewn across the ceiling, over the same deep purple, was the solar system March's mom, Candy, had freehanded. She was a graphic artist who worked from home.

"I'm busy," March grumbled.

"It can't be homework, because it's Saturday, and you said Mr. Carter doesn't give homework on the weekends."

"I can still be busy even though I don't have homework."

I walked toward him, pulled the contents from my manila folder, and dropped them dramatically onto the corner of his desk, except I missed and the pages fluttered to the floor. I bent to pick them up, trying to reorder the four printouts. "Operation: Expose James Crowley. Coordinator of Spying: Kazuko Jones. Director of Computer Hacking: March Winters."

I handed him the stack, which felt thin after the failed dramatic reveal. He shuffled through them and scoffed. "So you found his Facebook page, his LinkedIn profile, his wife's obituary, and his address, which we already knew?"

"That's why you're the Director of Computer Hacking. I can't do this without you."

"Do what? Mr. Crowley is harmless."

"Then prove me wrong." I dropped onto a beanbag covered in rocket-printed fabric. "Besides, you love an excuse to hack anyone. Consider this an exercise in Operation: College Entrance. Scratch that. Operation: College Scholarship Extravaganza!"

Now that I thought about it, March's eyes were probably extra-wide because everything he saw was lit by the MIT logo: the Massachusetts Institute of Technology, where he hoped to attend college someday. I knew what motivated March Winters, and you had to know people to work 'em.

March tilted his head to the side, considering. "It won't be hard, because he's old, and most old people don't know how to protect their computers. But it's still illegal."

"Dognapping is more illegal." I pushed up from the beanbag, hoping to spur March to action.

"Actually, in Colorado, dognapping is considered petty theft while computer hacking is a felony. So it's not more illegal."

Smarty-pants. But I couldn't ruin it with name-calling. March hated being called names.

"Well, it *should* be more illegal." I placed my hand on his shoulder. "Please, March. Do it for the puppies."

He shrugged me off. March didn't like to be touched.

"Do it for the puppies," he mimicked, his voice high and his face pinched.

"Is that a yes?"

He sighed, making a show of it. "That's a yes."

CHAPTER NINE

Mom sounded disappointed when I called to ask if I could stay at March's for a late-over that night.

"But we were going to watch *Goonies*," she said. Party Night Saturday was a serious Jones tradition at my house where Dad baked his famous Dorito casserole for dinner, and then, before the movie, Mom and I air-popped popcorn, covered it with real butter, and sprinkled chocolate chips on top. We watched the movie in my parents' room, upstairs, tucked into their California king-size bed, where I usually fell asleep between Mom and Dad, and Genki spent the evening whimpering from a doggie pad on the floor.

"Next week," I promised, feeling torn between

my detective work and one of my favorite family traditions.

"Don't tell me you're already too cool for your parents."

"Mo-o-o-m." I wanted to argue how mature I was but realized drawing her name out like that wasn't helping.

"Okay," she said, like she didn't want to hear it. "Have fun."

March and I ate pizza for dinner while watching *Napoleon Dynamite* in the basement. That's not even one of my favorite movies, but at the Winterses' house you had to vote for everything, and we were always outnumbered by the younger boys and Macy, March's thirteen-year-old sister. Maggie had taken May, Lakeview High freshman, to her first high school football game. Their parents, Marshall and Candy, were on what they called a House Date, eating takeout by candlelight in the dining room upstairs. That's why we all crowded onto the buckling furniture in their basement, kneeing and elbowing each other while we tried to balance loaded paper plates on our laps.

After we finished eating, March and I threw our trash in the kitchen garbage and tiptoed past the dining room. March's parents had pushed their chairs away from the table, where they leaned into each other, talking softly. Takeout boxes and fancy china plates spotted with mounds of chow mein cluttered the table. Hopper sat patiently at Mr. Winters's side, his nose waving at some phantom smell as he waited for them to gift him the leftovers.

"Oh, all right!" Mr. Winters put the two fancy plates on the floor, and Hopper pushed them around the dining room as he licked them clean. I noticed another empty dish stuck under one of the chairs. Hopper also knew how to work people.

I followed March back to his room, where he cracked his knuckles before settling in at the desk.

"Okay," he said. "If we're going to hack Mr. Crowley, we need his e-mail address. Does your route list have that?"

"No." I took the stack from March and pulled out my route list, which only included customer names, addresses, and phone numbers. I waved the list at him.

March pointed at me, even though there was no one else in the room. "*You* need to call him and ask for it. Otherwise this will never work."

"Why?" I balled my hands into fists. Computer hacking was Phase One, which was low risk and required no contact. If I called Geezer, he might figure out I was onto him. What if he tracked me down?

"Because I need to send him an e-mail with an attachment. If I do this right, once he clicks on it, the attachment will run an application connecting his computer to mine. On his end, it won't look like anything happened. But on my end, I'll have access to his desktop, and we can see all the stuff old people do with their computers."

"I have to talk to him? Like, for real?"

"How else do we get his e-mail address? Just tell him you're his paper carrier, and the *Denver Chronicle* needs to add his e-mail address to their records so they can send paperless notifications or something."

"Can't you do it? You sound so smart."

"No way," he said. "This is your crazy idea, Kazu, not mine. You either get his e-mail address or we cancel Operation: Expose James Crowley."

He handed me his phone. I turned it over in my palm a couple times, thinking of the dog food receipt stuffed into the bottom of Geezer's recycled newspaper bags.

Then I thought of Mrs. Tanner crying at her doorway because Barkley was missing. Because I had *let* Barkley go missing. What were the chances that the one person who could have stopped Barkley's dognapping in the first place would find the receipt and be given a chance to bring Barkley home?

I dialed Geezer's number.

CHAPTER TEN

He picked up after the first ring.

"Hello?" He said it like "yellow." His voice was warm and deep, like a grandpa's.

"Hi," I said. "This is your papergirl, and the *Denver Chronicle* needs your e-mail address for their records. We want to start sending electronic notifications." My words tumbled out, and I wondered if he could even understand me. I didn't sound nearly as professional as March had when he suggested this approach.

"What's your name again?"

My name? I shouldn't give him my name, right? Maybe a fake name would be best. "Kazuko Jones," I said, unable to think of a good alias on the spot.

"And what are these electronic notifications?"

Why hadn't I put the phone on speaker so that March could help me?

Okay. Why would a newspaper send electronic notifications? I thought of all the boring stuff I had seen in Mom's in-box. "You know, bills and newsletters and Christmas cards?" March slapped his forehead.

"That makes sense." Geezer rattled off his e-mail address, and I wrote it next to his phone number on my route list.

"Thank you very much," I said.

"Oh, and Costco?"

I grimaced at his attempt to say my name. "Yes?"

"Would you mind bagging my papers instead of rolling them with rubber bands? When you deliver that early, they get all dewy from the frost."

"Sure. Of course."

"Also," he said as I moved to hang up, "I've noticed you deliver papers with your dog. Be careful out there. Denver pets are going missing, and I'd hate for my papergirl to lose her sidekick." He chuckled like that was a real knee-slapper. Stupid Geezer.

"Bye," I said, punching the END button.

March jumped out of his chair and double high-fived me. We hooted for a bit before he said, "Christmas cards?"

"I did it. That's what matters." But I laughed with him, glad it was over.

"Okay, I'll do a little hacking and then send the e-mail. If he opens the attachment, we're in business."

I nodded, replaying the phone conversation in my mind. Who jokes about missing pets? My face flushed, my cheeks tingling painfully. And just as quickly, relief flooded my body because Geezer thought his papergirl's name was Costco.

March and I crouched behind the school a few yards from the bus turnout to work on a Rulebook for Operation: Expose James Crowley (aka Geezer). The sun hung low in a clear sky, and the air had a cold bite to it. Pinched between two electrical boxes, we talked as kids ran back and forth across the soccer field, their squeals echoing behind them. Some already wore scarves and mittens, their breath cloudy in the morning chill.

The bell would ring soon, so we worked quickly, whispering to avoid being overheard. I opened my Sleuth Chronicle, picking a clean sheet behind all the data and articles about the Denver Dognapping Ring, and began to take notes. When I finished, I handed the notebook to March, and he read the list of rules aloud:

1. Never talk about the operation in public.
2. Do not share operation intel with anyone else, most importantly, parents.
3. Keep all operation documents locked in March's metal Christmas safe.
4. To avoid suspicion, do not communicate directly with Mr. Crowley (except for when we asked for his e-mail because we had to).
5. Involve police when we have hard evidence.
6. Do not do anything that will get us killed.

I nodded. That sounded about right, although I realized that heroes were often required to break rules when lives were at stake. But this was not the time to have that conversation with March, who loved rules, to-do lists, and numbered tasks.

March said Mr. Crowley still hadn't opened the attachment he had sent Saturday night from a dummy e-mail account. "Some people don't check their e-mail very often," he explained as I shoved the notebook back into my pack.

"But how do you know he hasn't already opened the e-mail and ignored the attachment?"

"Because I have an app that tells me when the e-mails I send are opened. He should at least open the e-mail, don't you think?"

The bell rang. We stood and swatted the dirt

from our pants before swinging backpacks over shoulders.

"What did the e-mail say?"

March's voice was a whisper. "Subject line: Denver East High School Fiftieth Reunion. 'Dear James Crowley, We are planning a fiftieth reunion for the Denver East High School graduating class of 1969. Please click the attachment below to RSVP. Thanks and hope to see you this summer! Signed, Albert Parker, 1969 Class President.'"

It turned out that my puny stack of papers had helped after all. James Crowley listed Denver East High School in his educational history on Facebook. It didn't take much research to discover that Albert Parker was the class president in 1969, the year Crowley had graduated, although neither one of us had been able to determine whether or not Albert Parker was still alive. We decided to take a chance, and March created the dummy e-mail account in Albert's name; we hoped this would increase the odds that Geezer would open the e-mail and then the attachment.

"Now we wait?" I asked.

We entered the school's foyer. March walked in a straight line, each foot placed in the middle of a tile. I had never seen him step on a crack, like, ever.

March nodded. "I'll be alerted as soon as he opens the attachment, and then I can find all the dirt on

Mr. Crowley. Like whether he recycles, cheats at solitaire, or tips his papergirl." He snorted, and I glared at him.

"He doesn't, by the way," I said. "How can you trust an old guy who doesn't tip his papergirl?"

We stopped at the top of the stairs. Kids swarmed around us.

"Maybe that's exactly why you *can* trust this old guy," March said. "Because he doesn't tip the papergirl who's spying on him."

I shoved my fists deep into my pockets, scrambling for a biting comeback. "We're breaking rule number one: Never talk about the operation in public."

"Dang it!" March said, and I knew he would fret about that broken rule all day.

March slunk to Mr. Carter's class, and I smirked as I turned in the opposite direction.

CHAPTER ELEVEN

Mrs. Hewitt had Madeleine and me sing through the song once before she critiqued our performance. It was about two kids walking to school, looking at bugs, learning the alphabet, making friends. The title came from the chorus, "I can tell that we are going to be friends." We both held our limp sheet music and sang without enthusiasm.

I glared at Mrs. Hewitt when she wasn't looking, my chest tight like a fist. No one in the fifth grade cared about the things in this song, especially not Madeleine Brown. I looked sideways at her as we sang about a new school year: "Back to school, ring the bell, brand-new shoes, walking blues . . . I can tell that we are going to be friends."

Madeleine rolled her eyes.

We finished the song, and Mrs. Hewitt plunked her hands on the keys, the angry, discordant sound echoing in the music room. We faced the backside of the piano as she bent over the keyboard, shaking her head.

"Ladies." She let out a long sigh. "That was pretty horrible."

"She keeps messing me up," Madeleine complained, nodding her head in my direction. "She sings really loud, and sometimes it's not even the right—"

"I'm singing all the right words," I cut her off before she could finish. "And *she's* not singing loud *enough*."

"You're both singing like kids who just had fillings put in all their teeth." Mrs. Hewitt walked around the piano to stand in front of us and mimicked, "'We are going to be friends,'" only her mouth opened and shut like a puppet's and each word hit the same note.

"When you sing, it must come from your heart." She hit her chest with her fist, turned her head toward the ceiling, and closed her eyes. Madeleine and I exchanged glances.

"You should sing about friendship with joy and gratitude." She circled us. "You should push the words from your stomach with such force that they ring from your lips. Just imagine. What would you do without friends?"

Well, I thought. Madeleine would have a tougher

time bullying people, that's for sure. I side-eyed her, and she mirrored my glare.

"You may not like each other very much," Mrs. Hewitt said, returning to her place in front of the piano. "But you can think about all the friends you *do* like while singing this song. Let's give it a try."

We tried three more times, and Mrs. Hewitt became more dissatisfied with each attempt. When we'd finished the chorus for the last time, she closed the piano and walked out of the music room. She didn't even bother to turn around when she said, "I'll see you both again next week!"

I raked a neat pile of orange leaves in the corner of Mrs. White's yard, which was across the street from our house. Every year she paid me to clear the leaves and then, when it snowed, shovel her drive. This year the leaves from her aspen had fallen early due to an extra-dry summer, and she had waved me over on my way home from school.

She sat on her porch, talking while she watched me work. "My husband, see," she said, "never slowed down. He kept up on all the maintenance around here, and when he passed, I had to get help, being a bent old hag by then." She chuckled, her voice gravelly. Mrs. White told me this same story every year.

She was a small old lady, not much taller than me, hunched at the waist and shuffling with a cane when she walked. Her husband died three years ago, when I was eight. I had done odd jobs for her ever since, like Allen, her handyman, who mowed her lawn, hung her Christmas lights, cleaned and oiled her shake roof, stained her wood fence, and even rolled out her trash can every Monday morning on garbage day.

I nodded as she talked and I raked, knowing that I got paid just as much for being polite as I did for finishing the job. But when I saw March jogging toward me, a manila folder clutched in one hand, I rushed to gather the leaves and push them deep into the garbage can she used for yard clippings. He got there in time to help me pick up stray leaves and then drag the can toward the garage.

"Well, hello there, March!" Mrs. White called, cupping her hands around her mouth. March smiled back stiffly and waved like a robot. "Whatcha got there?" She nodded at the folder, which he had set in the grass while he helped me finish.

"Nothing," he said too quickly. And then, after a beat, "Homework."

She smiled, her lips curled around big square teeth.

"It's good to see kids work. Yard work. Homework. It's healthy. Turns you into good citizens."

"Do you want me to put the can back in your garage?" I asked. Her code—1065—probably hadn't changed since they first installed the garage door. As I asked, a DineWise van—a meal delivery service for old people—pulled into her driveway. They did good business in our neighborhood.

"I got it." Mrs. White leaned on her cane with one hand and waved the garage-door opener at me with the other, pushing the button for emphasis. "Thanks, Kazuko! I'll walk your money over later."

The garage door creaked open, and the truck pulled in. March bounced next to me like he was going to pee himself.

"Let's go," he whispered, grabbing the folder from the grass and darting across the street ahead of me.

"Bye, Mrs. White," I called over my shoulder, but she had already slipped into the garage and shut the door.

When we walked into my house, Genki jumped on March, nearly knocking him over. We both got a good sniff-down as we kicked off our shoes in the entryway. "Do you want a snack?" Mom called to us from the kitchen. Even though she worked at the museum part-time, she spent the rest of her time working from home so she could be here when I got back from school.

"We're fine," I called back as we ran up to my room, knowing she would throw something together for us, anyway.

March reeled back as soon as he opened the door, as if he'd stepped into a wind tunnel. Genki sat down behind him, cocking his head from side to side as he waited March out.

"Holy crap!" March said. His nose scrunched as he stood in my doorway.

I pushed him in, and he acted like I'd dropped him into a vat of Ebola virus.

"Disgusting! I can't work here." March hugged the manila folder to his chest, standing on the one clear spot of carpet in the middle of my bedroom, with piles of dirty clothes, used towels, books, and random junk around him. When we were younger, he would offer to clean my room for free because he said picking up such a huge mess made him all tingly inside. But once we started detecting together, he preferred solving mysteries to sanitizing my room.

"Come on," I said, stepping over the obstacles and sitting on my unmade bed. Genki jumped up next to me and began digging around the blankets to make himself a nest. "It's not going to kill you. I mean, look at me."

"Your immune system is probably superhuman by

now, building a tolerance to who knows what's in here."

I stood and swiped a fleece blanket from Genki, who was still digging, and shook it onto the top of my bed before smoothing the corners for March. "Sit down. My room is *cluttered*, not *dirty*. There are no biohazards here."

He blew out an annoyed breath before sitting down next to me. Genki continued to paw at the bottom of my bed, fluffing up the perfect resting spot.

"So what is it?" I cut my eyes to the folder squared on March's lap.

"Oh!" His eyes lit up like a pinball machine after a killer shot. "Mr. Crowley opened the attachment today, and I was able to hack his desktop."

CHAPTER TWELVE

March kicked away the junk surrounding my bed and opened the folder, laying printouts on the floor. Genki, finally settled in a mound of fabric, jumped from the bed and sniffed at the sheets of paper before plopping down on top of them. March groaned.

"Move." I pointed back at my bed. Genki stood up slowly, like a grandpa dog, and jumped back to his blanket nest, which he began to rearrange even though it hadn't been disturbed.

March straightened the printouts and said, "You were right. There's some suspicious stuff on Crowley's computer." He pointed to the sheets of paper, talking faster and faster as he explained. "Mr. Crowley has bookmarked every article about the missing dogs. He also book-marked a website that explains the benefits of different dog breeds—which ones are naturally more aggressive, which ones are more teachable, which breeds cost the most. His order history from Amazon included a black ski mask, a black jacket, a window tinting kit, and three hundred feet of utility rope. His web cache included a website teaching how to remove microchips from dogs. And his bank account lists a bunch of deposits from a local company called Seenile Gizmos. I looked it up—something to do with *geriatric lifestyle components*."

I squinted at him.

"That one's not suspicious, just weird."

"He's our guy," I said. "What else could it all mean?" My mind got stuck on the detail about removing micro-chips, which store all the information a shelter needs to locate a dog's owner. When we got Genki, Dad had explained how they would shoot the microchip from a needle into his back, just like a vaccination. He prom-ised it wouldn't hurt. But removing one was probably more complicated. It was probably bloodier. Now the image of Barkley cowering on the red-stained floor of the dognapping van trailed goose bumps down my back.

"I don't know," March said. "Maybe he's interested in the dognappings, and the rest is a coincidence."

"It's just a coincidence that he's buying tons of dog

food and wants to know how to remove microchips? What about his order history?" I picked up the article about the dognappings, the same one in my Sleuth Chronicle, and skimmed for information on Barkley's disappearance. Had the windows on the dirty van been dark? "A black jacket is one thing, but a ski mask and a tinting kit? Who needs dark windows in Colorado?"

March shrugged. "We need more evidence before we can tell the police. Besides, they'd arrest me or something for all this." He motioned to the papers spread on the floor.

"You're right," I said. "We need more evidence!" I slammed a fist on my bed, and Genki startled.

"Oh no," March said. "What are you thinking?"

"A little dumpster diving," I said, facing him. "Once you roll your garbage to the curb, it's public property, right? That means we won't be doing anything illegal."

"Only if you believe everything you see on TV."

"I think it's pretty legit," I said.

"Okay, then." March gathered all the printouts and slid them into the folder. "Why don't we ask our parents if we can go through our neighbor's garbage looking for evidence of a dognapping?"

I rolled my eyes. "That breaks rule number two."

"But sneaking out after dark to steal his garbage breaks rule number five."

"We can't get killed trolling through someone's trash. It's gross, not dangerous."

"Unless he really is a hardened criminal and catches us. And takes us away. And kills us."

"Janken pon?" I held my fist in an open hand.

March and I had resolved disputes using Rock-Paper-Scissors since we were six years old. I had taught him how to play, and for years after he thought the game was named after some guy named John Kempo. I hadn't realized it was called anything else because Mom had first taught it to me, I guess in one of her Japanese cultural moments, as "Janken pon." When March and I couldn't agree on something, one of us would say "Janken pon" and assume the position. It was the quickest way to reach an agreement.

"Really, Kazu?"

I raised my right fist in the air over my left palm.

"All right," he grumbled.

"Janken pon," we said as we beat our fists into our palms.

"Scissors beats paper." March snapped at my hand with two fingers.

"Janken pon."

"Paper beats rock." I slapped his fist with my open hand.

"Janken pon."

"And rock beats scissors!" I punched March's two

stared me down. "This year, I'd like you to be something *other* than a detective."

I tipped my chin toward Mom. "Is that a suggestion or a requirement?"

"A requirement."

I stood so fast I knocked the bar chair to the ground. Genki scrambled to his feet, struggling to find his footing on the hardwood floor.

"That's not fair," I whined. "It's just a costume—it's pretend."

"You're not pretending, Kazuko." The insides of her eyebrows dipped low, and she eyed the fallen chair. "You haven't been pretending for a while, and if it doesn't stop, you're going to get hurt. It's my job to prevent that from happening."

"By making me dress up like a cat?"

"By helping you change your focus to something else."

"Fine!" I barked, backing away from the counter while avoiding the chair. "I'll be a zombie or a vampire or a rotting corpse."

Her face contorted for a second before settling into a smile. "You'll have to choose just one, Kazu."

I stormed up the steps to my room, stomping as hard as I could manage without stepping on Genki, who cowered around my feet.

CHAPTER THIRTEEN

March and I dangled our feet through the railing of his tree house. It spanned two oak trees in his family's backyard with a shelter the size of a rich person's shed on one tree and a catwalk connecting it to a smaller shed on the next. His dad had spent Maggie's entire childhood building it, and it still wasn't finished—the platform around the second tree was missing half a safety railing.

"When can we raid Geezer's garbage?" I asked.

"I don't know about this, Kazu," March said, clutching his metal Christmas safe like it would roll off his lap. "We could get in big trouble if anyone catches us. Or worse—maybe they'd kidnap us and put us in dog kennels with the rest of their stolen animals."

I had ridden my bike to March's house before dinner to plan Mission: Geezer's Garbage Raid. March's bedroom door had been open, and he jumped when I knocked on it. He claimed he was engrossed in a tutorial on coding, but I knew he was nervous about the mission.

"Maybe I can convince Mom to let me do the paper route with you one day," I said. "I could tell her you've finally agreed to train as a sub, and we'll ride our bikes. No one will see us then." The hardest thing about having a paper route was finding a substitute when we went out of town; Mom would be so excited about having a backup sub she wouldn't suspect a thing.

"But it'll be dark, and quiet," he said. "What if someone hears us?"

Something took flight in my chest, but I ignored it.

"You'd be surprised how deeply everyone sleeps," I said. "Once, I crashed my bike into two garbage cans on Summer Glen Drive and no one heard me."

He looked at me, one eyebrow raised.

"Seriously. The other day I hit your front door with the paper and no one woke up—not even *you*."

March studied the top of his safe with the operation documents locked inside. He shrugged.

"I don't want to pressure you or anything, but Barkley's been missing for over a week. If we don't hurry, there will be no information for Geezer to toss."

March sighed, setting the safe down next to him. "What are you going to be for Halloween?"

He was trying to change the subject, and his question stung a bit as I remembered Mom telling me I couldn't be Velma. "A zombie." I tried not to let my disappointment distract me. "And you're going to be Steve Jobs for the second year in a row—"

"Actually," he interrupted, "it's currently a toss-up between Steve Jobs and Payback, an obscure Marvel vigilante that used to work with the Punisher. . . ."

"So," I said, "it's a geek-off."

"You're not going to be a detective?" he asked.

I sighed. I was hoping mom would be horrified by the idea and would finally agree to let me dress up as a detective. Instead, she had looked at me with her perfect Moker Face—Mom Poker Face—and said, "That sounds wonderful. Just remember the no-gore rule for school."

I answered March, "Mom won't let me be a detective anymore. Not even for pretend." I tried to get our conversation back on track. "When are we going to do the garbage raid?"

"Did you not just hear yourself? About your mom forbidding detective work, real or pretend?"

I glared at him, and I could swear it made my eyes burn. "Barkley's gone because of me. I've got to get her back."

"Okay, okay," he said. "When?"

"Monday morning. The garbage will be on the curb. We should wear black."

March's shoulders slumped, and his chin nearly touched his chest.

"It'll be fun." I patted his knee. "You'll see."

I pushed my fear deep into my stomach, where it weighed me down like an anchor.

The next couple days dragged. Mom continued to drive me on my route. March spent afternoons overachieving on his homework while I avoided mine. And Dad ordered me green face paint and a plastic brain as a prop for my Halloween costume.

My anxiety about our next mission grew until Friday morning when Geezer finally left me a tip. I sat in the car after the route and studied the note he had taped to his door while Mom put away the rubber bands and gathered all the newspaper garbage.

Kazuko Jones,

I contacted the Denver Chronicle, and they gave me your full name and recommended I leave any personalized gifts for you at my door. Thank you for bagging my newspapers to prevent the Colorado frost from dampening them. I appreciate all your hard work delivering my papers very early in the morning. Also, I asked the paper when I could expect to receive "electronic notifications" and they didn't know what I was talking about. That's strange, now, isn't it?

Thanks again for all your hard work,
James Crowley

Along with the note he had attached an orange newspaper bag to his door holding a single PAYDAY candy bar.

CHAPTER FOURTEEN

"**T**hat was nice of him," Mom said, reading over my shoulder.

I folded the note in half and shoved it in my pocket.

"What's he talking about—'electronic notifications'?"

I shrugged. "I have no idea." All the warmth drained from my cheeks, and my chest tightened.

Mom got out of the car and went back into the house through the garage. Genki waited as I stayed behind to sort another collection of recycled newspaper bags, the note hot in my pajama pocket.

As if he knew something was wrong, Genki sat at my feet, whimpering like he did around big groups of people. I patted his head, trying to calm him, but my own fears distracted me, and I soon found myself missing his head completely and pawing at the air, which only made Genki whine louder.

Was Geezer really grateful for the work I did, or was he mad that I had made up the story about the electronic notifications in order to get his e-mail address? And did he realize that it was all a trick to hack his computer?

While I wanted to believe the note was innocent and only pointed out a simple misunderstanding, I couldn't help but worry that he was onto us. I paced the garage, taking deep breaths while I counted slowly. Genki followed, trying to lick my fingers on the move.

The only person I could tell about the note—March—would be so freaked-out that he would cancel our mission. No amount of Janken would convince him otherwise, and I couldn't complete this mission on my own. We'd lose our only chance at gathering evidence that could prove James Crowley was the Denver Dognapper. I was *not* going to let that happen.

After school, Mrs. White had me weed her flower patch and spray down her driveway for five dollars. She sat on the porch and chatted while I worked, the afternoon warmer than usual for October. Her husband was always the main topic of conversation.

"Did I ever tell you Nile was an entrepreneur? Always inventing gadgets that could make life easier."

I nodded as I added to the weed pile at my side.

"If I had the money, I'd produce all those gadgets and open a store where people like me could come and find contraptions that would improve their lives. In fact, just between you and me, I'm working on opening up a little shop in his remembrance, named after my Nile."

She took a long swig from her iced tea and then shook the glass; the ice clinked inside.

"I'm impressed with your work ethic, Kazuko," she said. "Is that a Japanese thing? Because I don't see many kids your age who work as hard as you do."

The question needled my chest. It sounded like a compliment but didn't feel like one. "My friend March is doing homework right now, and it's Friday. *And* his teacher doesn't even give homework on Fridays." I grabbed a pile of weeds and dropped them into the plastic bin. I had already finished spraying down her driveway. "He works hard, too, doing different things. I'm saving for an iPad."

"And you deliver papers every morning." She sucked air through her teeth while shaking her head. Even though she said lots of weird stuff about me being Japanese, Mrs. White was one of my favorite customers because the first of every month she always left a ten-dollar tip in her newspaper box. "That's discipline."

"I guess."

"Did you know they used to make newspaper carriers collect payments? It was part of their job. Every month, our paperboy Sean would show up at our door, sheepish as ever, asking for six dollars and twenty-eight cents. He looked like Oliver Twist with his hands held out. *Please, sir, I want some more.*" She held her own hands out, cupped like a beggar's, and spoke the last part in a British accent. I looked up at her from the flower patch. Mrs. White and Mrs. Hewitt would make great friends.

"Anyway," she continued, "can you imagine not getting paid until you collected all the money the newspaper charged every person on your route?"

"No," I said, going after a dandelion cluster with the weed puller. "Mom hates school fund-raisers where we have to collect money door-to-door. I wouldn't be doing my paper route if we had to do that." I sat back on my haunches, imagining the *Denver Chronicle* reinstating that policy. We would quit, and I could sleep in, poor but well rested.

"Anyway," Mrs. White said. "They stopped that after the girl disappeared."

I dropped the weed puller. "What?"

"Oh, you wouldn't have heard—it was way before you were even born. Nineteen ninety-three, I think."

"A papergirl disappeared?"

"Her name was Loralee Sanders. She was collecting

money in Clinton, suburb up the road? And they think this crazy bat—faithful *Chronicle* subscriber—kidnapped her."

I stood, my hands hanging limp at the end of my arms. "What? That really happened?"

"It sure did. And you know how they found him? She had a dog that followed her everywhere, and when she disappeared, that puppy never left the man's yard. His neighbors became suspicious of the guy who had to fend off an angry dog every time he set foot outside his house. Think it was a Doberman mix." She stood and studied her porch light, covered in spiderwebs. "Maybe you can swing by tomorrow and clean these up." Mrs. White waved her cane at the webbing spotted with dead gnats and mosquitoes.

"Wait a minute," I said. "The missing papergirl? That's a scary story you tell other papergirls around Halloween, right?"

"Oh no, dear." She turned around and faced me, her hands clasped in front of her. "That happened. And afterward, there was a real outcry—the whole community came down hard on the *Chronicle*. I mean, who expects children to act as bill collectors? Ludicrous."

I turned back to the flower patch and collected all the weeds I had pulled, dropping them into the trash bin. "I gotta go." I felt dizzy, and my entire body shivered.

"Kazuko, sweetheart?" Mrs. White called after me as

I crossed the street. "Please come back. I didn't mean to frighten you. That's long since over, dear, and you don't have a thing to worry about."

The thought of interrupting my paper route to rummage through Geezer's garbage didn't seem quite as harmless anymore. And clearly having a guard-dog extraordinaire wouldn't guarantee my safety.

"I'm okay," I yelled at her, not looking back.

But I was not okay. Not at all.

CHAPTER FIFTEEN

A quick internet search proved that Mrs. White was right. The only thing she had gotten wrong was that it all happened in 1991 and not 1993. Plus, the dog was a shepherd mix about Genki's size. And even though that looney probably kidnapped Loralee Sanders more than twenty-five years ago, the information still made me sick.

I closed down the computer and went to my room. Genki followed me into bed, and I took a blanket and made a tent over us. Genki nuzzled my ear while I tried to take a nap, but my stomach was all woozy. Dad knocked on my door after he got home from work; I had ignored Mom's attempts to lure me from my room, but he was more persistent.

He pulled the blanket down and poked my ribs with his finger. "Well, your reflexes are working okay."

"I'm not sick," I said. "I just don't feel like doing anything." I turned toward the wall.

He sat next to me on the bed, and the depression in the mattress pulled on my body like a magnet. Genki rolled even closer to me, arching his back so that his chest was in my face.

Dad rubbed my shoulder. "Would you like to go to dinner at the Golden Buckle for an impromptu Party Night Friday?"

The Golden Buckle was my favorite restaurant, and not because of the barbecue beef sandwiches with the best sauce on the planet, but because they had a little bucking bronco only kids could ride. My personal best was forty-two seconds; any other night I would have jumped at the chance to beat it.

"I'm not really hungry," I said.

"Okay, Bug, this is where you tell me what's *really* wrong. That's our thing, remember? You tell me anything, and I stay cool as a cucumber."

Dad and I made that deal in the second grade when I was afraid to tell Mom I swallowed her pachinko ball, a souvenir she brought back years ago from her first trip to Japan with Dad. The pachinko ball was a silver orb the size of a tiny marble and, according to Mom, was used in

Japan's version of slot machines. I had put it in my mouth to give it a quick taste and accidentally swallowed it. Only after imagining the pachinko ball knocking around my gut like the insides of a pinball machine, building to what was sure to be a painful and slow death, did I finally tell my parents.

Mom freaked out. We went to the emergency room, got some X-rays, and then the doctor told us it looked like the pachinko ball had already made its way to the resting place of dead goldfishes and swallowed nickels. Later that night, Dad pulled me aside and promised that if there was anything stressing me out, I could tell him and he would never yell at me—which was good, because sometimes Mom could get worked up about stuff.

I rolled over and looked at him. "Do you think the dognapper is dangerous?"

"What do you mean?"

"I mean, do you think the dognapper would ever hurt *people*?"

He sighed and then sat silent for a second. When he finally spoke, his words came out slowly. "I think the dognapper is selfish and trying to make money in a horrible way, but I don't think he'd hurt people."

"But we don't know, right? If someone tried to stop him, he could become dangerous, don't you think?"

"Maybe," he answered. "But we don't need to worry

about that. The police are doing their best to find the dognapper, and when they do, Barkley will go back to the Tanners."

I tugged at the fringe on my fleece blanket. "I hope so."

"I know you're afraid, Bug," he said. "But you know you're safe with us, right? Your mother and I aren't going to let anything happen to you. Or Genki." He reached across me and scratched Genki's tummy.

I nodded, and I knew he meant it. But Dad couldn't protect me from a mission he knew nothing about and a potential dognapper who also happened to be the creepiest guy on my paper route. Maybe it would be best if March and I canceled Operation: Expose James Crowley.

What if that also meant Lobster was never returned to CindeeRae Lemmings or Barkley stopped being the Tanners' practice baby? What if that meant more dogs went missing when March and I could have stopped it?

"Come on," Dad said, pulling me up and slinging me over his shoulder. "Let's go to dinner, watch a movie, and remember what it's like to just be a kid, okay?"

"Okay," I said, knowing I would have to pretend.

"Mom, guess what?" I asked, trying to sound natural. It was Sunday morning, and we huddled on the sectional in our living room. Mom and Dad read the paper while I made a list in the Sleuth Chronicle of everything March and I needed for Mission: Geezer's Garbage Raid.

"What?" She leaned against Dad's chest as she turned the page, holding the paper at arm's length as she did. They were cuddling in the corner of the couch while I stretched out on the sofa's long arm. Genki lay on the floor in front of me while I patted his back with one slippered foot. Lazing around our living room was a Sunday morning tradition that sometimes lasted until lunch. Usually I hated the quiet, slow pace of Sundays, but today I had a plan that depended on Mom being chill.

"March wants to train as a sub." I pretended to concentrate on my notebook, and the words blurred together as I kept my expression blank.

She folded the paper in half and set it on her lap. "Really? For three years that boy has refused to sub your route, and suddenly he has a change of heart?" She sat up and tossed a look over her shoulder at Dad. "It's still dark at six in the morning, and I know Candy and Marshall aren't going to drive him around that early."

I looked to the ceiling, posing thoughtfully. "Something about turning eleven has changed us, Mom." March's birthday was two days after mine, at the end of August, making us the oldest kids in our class. While we had been eligible for kindergarten, having turned five less than a week before school started, both our mothers had apparently been afraid we were too socially immature. That meant one more year of intensive preschool before we both endured the most boring year of kindergarten ever. Maybe that's why March and I had gotten into record-breaking trouble that year, and also why Principal Smith recommended we never share a classroom at Lincoln Elementary again. And we hadn't.

Mom studied my face. "Really? Like how?"

"Like we're not afraid of the dark, and we like earning our own money, and being responsible for something." I tapped my pencil on the notebook.

She nodded. "Okay. Tell him we'll pick him up at six fifteen tomorrow morning."

"But . . ."

Mom had already opened the paper again but dropped it to peek over the top. "But what?"

My mind scrambled to think of a reason Mom shouldn't be driving us on the paper route tomorrow. "But when *he* subs, March won't have anyone to drive him. It's better if we ride our bikes so he can get used to that."

This time she set the paper on her lap, and it covered her like an apron. "Kazu, we're just trying to be extra safe!"

"And we will be—March will be with me. And Genki—he'll protect us." Genki sat up and looked at me, waiting for the punch line. I grabbed his ears and turned his face toward my parents, hiding behind his head and speaking in a deep, raspy voice. "Look how scary I am."

Dad tried not to laugh while Mom shook her head at me. "You and March are still kids, and Genki, intimidating as he may be, is a dog and the target of dognappers. He may not be able to protect you from a predator."

I imagined us staring down a T. rex on Colonial Avenue, right outside Geezer's house, Genki going all were-monster.

"Then let me take the phone. I'll text if anything happens."

Dad leaned forward. "Kazu," he said in his deep, serious voice, "I agree with your mother. You and March are smart and mature kids, but Genki is a rare dog—he'd be a real catch for this dognapping ring."

"But how's March going to practice if we don't do the route by bike?"

Mom and Dad looked at each other. Getting a second sub would make family trips much easier. Right now we had to plan around our only sub's schedule, and he was in high school and quickly losing interest in a paper route that only paid ten dollars a weekend. And while it wasn't very likely March would change his mind about subbing once we completed the mission, I could still pretend he might.

"I'll drop you off at March's house and wait for you in the middle of Summer Glen Drive," Mom said, looking at

Dad as she spoke. He nodded. "But Genki will stay in the car with me. You can take the cell phone to call if there are any problems when you're out of sight. Otherwise, I'll be there to see you complete each loop of the route."

Summer Glen Drive was the center of my route's figure eight. From the middle of the block, you could see the corner of Geezer's house, where Colonial met Summer Glen, but not necessarily his driveway, where the garbage can would be. If I argued with her now, it would be suspicious—why would I care that much about biking my route with March when I had been relieved that she had volunteered to drive me last week?

"Okay," I said. "That works."

I snapped my notebook shut, stood up, and ran upstairs to my room, Genki trotting behind me. March and I would have to revise our plan.

CHAPTER SIXTEEN

March and I parked our bikes in the middle of Summer Glen Drive, studying the view of Geezer's house. It hadn't been hard to convince Mom that March was nervous about making his first paper route run in the dark and wanted to practice in the daylight, but she had made me keep Genki home.

Summer Glen was long and straight, intersected on each end by my street, Honeysuckle, on the bottom, and March's street, Colonial, at the top. My route covered both sides of four blocks, and when I delivered papers, I did half of my block before cutting over to March's on Morningside. All the streets on my route were lined with tall trees whose leaves had already turned orange and red. In the light of dusk it looked like they were on fire, shuddering in the breeze.

"You can't see his driveway from here," March said.

Not only was Geezer's house surrounded by trees, but the house across the street from his had a curve of shrubbery outlining the yard, which also blocked the view.

I whispered back. "If he doesn't put his garbage can at the end of his driveway—like if he rolls it closer to the stop sign—she might be able to see us, especially if she parks closer to his house."

March nodded. Unlike me, he was relieved my mother would be close enough to wave down should we run into danger. I'm sure he also hoped her presence might prevent us from braving the mission at all, making us both too nervous to act.

I folded my arms across my chest. Summer Glen Drive was the only road on my route with streetlamps, and the first lamp was a couple houses away from Colonial. I always complained about how dark my route was. As long as there wasn't a full moon, Geezer's house would be a black hole.

"Okay. We'll be fine," I concluded. I tried not to think about the note Geezer had left with my tip, or the fact that I was keeping it from March. He would worry—no, be paralyzed with fear—if he thought the old guy was onto us. And if I shared that story about Loralee Sanders, March would probably lose his lunch and run back home, leaving his bike in a heap on the side of Summer Glen Drive. Nope. I'd have to die with my secrets, a thought that had left my stomach in a jumble since Friday afternoon.

We rode through the first loop of the route, stopping again on Summer Glen Drive. From my basket, I pulled two small backpacks: one for March and one for me. I had gotten them from my years volunteering for the Zoo Crew. They were both yellow and had HIGHLAND ZOO printed on them in blocky white letters. "Inside your pack," I said, "is a ski mask, a headlamp, and a utility belt."

"Who am I, Batman?"

I ignored him. "We'll pretend we're carrying extra rubber bands, the route map, and our cell phones. And we're not really pretending, because that stuff's in there with the spy gear."

"What's on the utility belt?"

I opened the pack and held it within view, not wanting to draw the belts into the open and make passersby nervous. Each belt was a canvas number I'd found in Dad's old Boy Scout supplies. To each I had attached a flashlight, a pocketknife, mini binoculars, and a kazoo, in case we really did have to get Mom's attention.

I whispered, pointing at each item, "Flashlight, pocketknife, binoculars, kazoo."

"Why do we need a pocketknife?" March's voice was high and shrill.

"Shhhh!" I zipped the pack shut. "For protection. Just in case."

March nodded solemnly, taking the pack from me and slinging it over his shoulders.

I continued, "We need to wear black and keep the headlamps on our heads, but only turn them on when we're looking through his trash. Otherwise, Mom might see the beams and come check things out."

"Are you sure about this, Kazu?"

"Listen," I said. "If we don't find anything tomorrow, I'll drop it. We'll forget about the note and the weird stuff on Geezer's computer. Operation over."

"Promise?"

"Promise."

March climbed onto his rickety ten-speed—his dad's old bike—and rode toward Colonial, where Geezer's house perched on the corner. He wobbled as he went.

"We'll see you tomorrow at six fifteen!" I yelled after him, and he waved back, keeping his face forward.

CHAPTER SEVENTEEN

Mom followed me in the car, my bike weaving in and out of the headlights and making spooky shadows on the pavement. She kept the windows up because once Genki saw I was riding my bike without him, he had begun to howl.

We stopped in front of March's house, and he came out through the garage before I even parked my bike. We both wore black, but March had a hoodie on that made everything but his face disappear into the darkness; he wheeled a bike next to him.

Mom pulled ahead and stopped when she was even with us. Soundlessly, we rode back to Summer Glen and stopped at the middle of the block, where she flipped a U-ey so that she'd see us when we rounded Colonial and made our way back toward the car. As she did, I could hear March's quick breaths, and the sound made my heart beat faster and my stomach flutter. Once she parked, Mom rolled down the window and handed me an armload of rolled newspapers. I layered them in my basket.

"Do both sides of Colonial and then come back to Summer Glen," Mom said, her voice low. "I'll be waiting right here. I'll follow you to Honeysuckle until you turn back up Morningside."

Genki stood with his front paws on the console, trying to push his bulk around her so he could stare me down. Even from where I stood, I could hear the sad hum from his chest. Mom pushed him back with her elbow. "That should be enough papers until you reach Summer Glen."

I couldn't wait to reach Summer Glen. Whatever we discovered, the mission would be over then, and we could go home.

Mom put the car into park and pulled out her phone. I gave March a side-eye before taking off ahead of him on my bike, realizing that while our main purpose was to complete the mission, I still had to deliver newspapers. We didn't have any time to lose since Mom would get worried if we didn't make it back to the car soon. Delivering to the five houses on March's street, including

Geezer's, would be the only time we were out of her sight.

I threw the paper onto the porch of the first subscriber on Colonial; March wobbled behind me.

We had three more papers to deliver before we reached Geezer's house. I opened my pack, took out the ski mask, and pulled it over my head. March did the same, watching me closely. Then I put the headlamp over the mask and buckled the utility belt. I handed March a paper but had to wait while he finished putting his gear on. "Toss this on your doorstep." I took off ahead of him and delivered the remaining two papers in a few seconds. I stopped at the last house and waited for March to catch up.

Across the street and two houses down was Geezer's house, which, as always, was a dark abyss, the trees and shrubbery blocking the view. March stopped next to me, his breath ragged and matching my own. While I wore a dark jacket and had warmed up as we rushed through the route, my arms were suddenly cold and prickly.

"We don't have much time," I whispered. Even though I could feel the urgency of our mission—our one chance—I stayed there, safe on my bike. We hadn't moved, yet my heartbeat grew stronger, and I heard it in my ears like the sound of a seashell pressed tight to my temple. I shook my head and handed March a newspaper from my basket. "You deliver the paper to his doorstep, and I'll start looking through the garbage. Remember, don't turn on your headlamp yet."

Slowly, we rode toward the house. Geezer's pickup was parked in the middle of his driveway, and I laid my bike down behind it while March parked his in the gutter, fighting with the kickstand to get it balanced. He walked toward the porch as I pulled open the lid on the garbage can and turned on my headlamp.

Inside were three white garbage bags tied at the top. I hadn't really thought about this part. We would have to tear through the bags to see what was inside. How often do people look into their trash cans after they roll them to the curb and before the garbage man comes? Not often, I guessed, although if Geezer did look, he would know someone had picked through it all. I didn't have time to think about it anymore; we had to hurry. I tore through the first bag.

A smell of rotten meat blew at me, and I pulled my head back instinctively. March stood next to me, turned on his headlamp, and looked inside. "What?" he asked.

"It's gross," I whispered.

I turned the bag over and watched meat scraps, egg-shells, paper napkins, plastic silverware, coffee grinds, envelopes, and DineWise boxes tumble out. I leaned over to grab the second bag but couldn't reach it. I stood on the curb, bent over the side of the can, and grabbed at the knot on top. As I went to pull it out, the can tipped into the grass and March's bike fell over, clanging when it hit the road. We both stood and waited as the sound echoed through the neighborhood. I got on my knees in the grass and reached into the can, now flat in the yard, and tore into the second bag.

"Kazu!" March whispered, pointing toward Summer Glen. Car lights shone from a distance. "I think it's your mom."

The second bag smelled worse than the first, but I pulled the trash out with my hands anyway and raked it toward me as I moved the headlamp over everything. In the last pile, stained by grease and some liquid, was a dog collar.

"We gotta go!" March said, and I shoved the collar inside my jacket and righted the can on the road.

"Take off the ski mask and the utility belt." The dog tags on the collar jingled beneath my jacket as I jogged to my bike. I pulled off my mask, headlamp, and utility belt and dropped them into my basket.

We met Mom in the middle of the street. She rolled down the passenger window and leaned across the console. "Where were you?"

"Just turning around," I said. "I think we missed the house that's back from vacation. Which one is it?"

Mom pulled the bundle-top from the dash and studied it under the interior light. March and I sat on our bikes, parked right at Colonial and Summer Glen, within eyeshot of Geezer's front door.

"It's two-seven-two-two," she said. "The house next door to March's."

"Okay," I said. "Then we got it right."

I began to pedal toward the next subscriber, even though I hadn't delivered to 2722 and would be charged a dollar for the miss.

CHAPTER EIGHTEEN

March and I had promised not to say anything about the dog collar until we could talk in private. I had slipped it to March at the end of the route to lock in the Christmas safe, and we went about our Monday like it was any other ordinary day. The cafeteria served rib-e-que for lunch. Officer Zig had us touch a smoker's lung for DARE. Lana Mesker threw up in reading. And I had one last detention music lesson with Madeleine Brown. Unless she messed everything up again.

Instead of having us sing this time, Mrs. Hewitt asked us to sit on the risers, handing us each a notebook and pencil.

"I would like you to make a list of ten things you like

most about your friends." She fidgeted with her phone, turning on a set of portable speakers as she talked. "Maybe even your *best* friend. For example, my best friend knows that when I've had a bad day, I like to vent about it over two large orders of chili fries."

Madeleine and I both snorted at that piece of information. I couldn't imagine ruining a perfectly good batch of fries with chili.

"I'll give you five minutes, so don't stew about it for too long."

Surrendering to the task, I thought about March and made my list, including things like:

- thinks I'm a good detective
- likes to laugh
- good listener
- doesn't make fun of me
- keeps secrets

I got so caught up in the assignment, my list had twelve items when Mrs. Hewitt called time.

"Nice work, ladies," she said. "Now. Switch lists."

For the first time since we'd started this detention craziness, we sang out in unison. "What?!"

"You heard me." She stood behind the music stand and folded her arms across her chest. "Switch lists."

I looked from Madeleine Brown to my open notebook and back again. Madeleine tore her page out and handed it to me like it was a math assignment she wanted me to grade. Either she wasn't worried about me seeing her list or she had mastered the Moker Face, too—Madeleine Poker Face. Trying to mimic her shrug, I passed my list to her.

"Now read what the other has written." Mrs. Hewitt's face almost wasn't big enough for the grin that stretched, clownlike, from one end of her molars to the other. She paced before the risers, nodding her head at her genius, no doubt.

Madeleine's list wasn't even serious:

- chews bubble gum
- follows me
- sits on my feet
- plays soccer
- licks my tears
- sings along to *"Achy Breaky Heart"*

My face burned as I remembered the first thing on my list: *thinks I'm a good detective.* I passed Madeleine's paper back without looking at her.

Thanks, Mrs. Hewitt, for ruining my life.

As if she could read my mind, Mrs. Hewitt packed up

her stuff and said, "Well, ladies. I think our work here is done."

Before she even dismissed us, Madeleine Brown had shot out from the room like her soccer cleats were on fire.

After school, March and I swung our legs from the top bunk in March's room; if I wanted to I could reach up and touch Pluto on the ceiling, a peppered orb the size of my fist. Barkley's pink collar lay between us on the galaxy bedspread. Her name tag, a pink doggie bone with swirly lettering, was faceup.

"Rule number five: Involve police when we have hard evidence," March said. "Barkley's dog collar is hard evidence."

I didn't say anything at first, thinking instead about the fight I'd had with Mom about my Halloween costume. If she didn't like the idea of me *pretending* to be a detective, what was she going to say when she found out we had dug through Geezer's garbage looking for clues?

"Barkley was in Geezer's house," I whispered. My stomach clenched, and I almost wished I had caught something from Lana Mesker in reading. "We have to tell the police. And our parents."

March nodded.

CHAPTER NINETEEN

March and I had both decided the chaos of his house would be too distracting. I asked him to bring his parents to my house at seven.

I had finished clearing the table when the doorbell rang. Mom and Dad shot each other a glance across the sink, where they were rinsing off dishes.

"Candy? Marshall?" Mom said when she opened the door.

March's parents smiled behind him while March looked like a reflection of me, his mouth crooked and eyebrows drawn together. His mom ruffled his hair and said, "March said he and Kazuko have something they need to tell us tonight. Sounded pretty ominous, so here we are."

His dad shrugged, and Mom opened the screen door for them while shooting me the what-have-you-done look. I ducked back into the kitchen to grab my Sleuth Chronicle from the counter.

"Make yourselves comfortable." Dad motioned them into the living room toward the black sectional. I caught up and followed them in. March and his parents sat on the long sofa while Mom and Dad claimed the corner—their favorite spot. I was the last one standing, and everyone looked at me like I was about to give a presentation. I clutched the Sleuth Chronicle to my chest. March nodded at me to get started—maybe I *was* giving a presentation.

March pulled Barkley's dog collar from inside his coat and pushed it across the coffee table toward me. I felt as if I had swallowed an ice cube whole, and the chill spread from my throat to my chest.

"What's going on, Kazu?" Mom asked, eyeing the dog collar.

I took a deep breath and let it out slowly, wondering if this was such a good idea after all. But there was no backing out now—I might as well get it over with.

"A few weeks ago, while doing the paper route, I found this at the bottom of a recycled bag." I opened the Sleuth Chronicle and pulled the receipt from where it rested in the middle, like a bookmark. I handed it to Mom. She studied it and passed the receipt to Dad. It traveled to the end of the couch, where March sat like a no-good lump. He handed it back to me.

"Soooo," I said, wishing March would jump in and tell the rest. We had already decided not to share any information about the hack on account of March possibly getting arrested. And no doubt his parents would be more forgiving of Mission: Geezer's Garbage Raid than they would Mission: Felony Hack. But still, a little help would have been nice.

Nope. Nothing.

"Because Geezer doesn't have a dog—"

Dad interrupted. "We don't call people names, Kazuko."

"Because *Mr. Crowley* doesn't have a dog, we thought the receipt was suspicious." I took a breath. "But we knew we'd need more evidence before anyone would believe us. That's why, today, when March and I did the paper route, we went through some of his garbage." All the parents looked like they had sucked a lemon slice, their faces pinched and sour. I rushed on, hoping to hasten my leap from troublemaker to heroine. "That's when we found this." I held up Barkley's dog collar. Mom snatched it from my hands.

The crease between her brows deepened as she studied the dog tags. "Do you know how dangerous that was?" I could barely hear her.

"I didn't think anyone would care about the receipt

unless we had more information," I said. "But that collar proves Barkley was in his house, right? How else could Mr. Crowley have gotten it? *He's* the Denver Dognapper."

The parents looked at each other, and March gave me a thumbs-up. I glared at him for making me tell the story by myself.

"Well," Dad said. "While this doesn't prove he did anything, we should definitely let the police know." He stood, walked to the kitchen, and grabbed his phone from the counter. When his call connected, he turned his back on the living room and lowered his voice to talk.

Mrs. Winters looked at her husband and said, "Do you really think James is behind all this? From what we know, he's just a lonely old hobbit."

March rolled his eyes. "*Hermit*, Mom. It's *hermit*."

When March spoke, Mom seemed to snap from a trance, and her laser-gaze drilled into me. "We need to talk about what you two did today." Her tone was calm and sharp, the worst combination.

I realized I still stood before them like I was giving a book report, my hands clasped in front of me. The room seemed to shrink.

"You got that right." March's dad spoke for the first time that night, his voice rumbling like Maggie's Satan voice.

"They're sending an officer over," Dad said, stepping

back into the living room. "They're going to want to talk to the kids."

I sat down next to March and held his hand, but only so that I could dig my fingernails into his palm. *He'd better help me this time.*

It only took fifteen minutes for a policeman to arrive. Officer Rhodes was taller than both Dad and Mr. Winters, with straw hair and a mole on the curve of his chin. Dad led him into the living room and invited him to sit on the teal leather armchair while I retold the story, except this time I sat on the couch between my parents. Officer Rhodes took notes, and then held out his hand for the receipt and Barkley's dog collar. I slid them both toward him across the coffee table, even though I wanted to say no.

When he finished all his questions, Officer Rhodes took a deep breath and leaned back in the chair. "I'm glad you reported this," he said. "But right now, all I can do is go to Mr. Crowley's house and see if he's willing to talk to me."

March and I nodded.

"But Mr. Crowley doesn't have to talk to me if he doesn't want to." Officer Rhodes leaned forward, tapping on his notebook with a pen. "He doesn't have to let me in his house; he doesn't have to show me his basement; he doesn't even have to open the door. He could yell 'Go away' after looking through his peephole, and I would have to go away."

"But you have Barkley's collar." This was the first time March had spoken voluntarily. His voice came out high and squeaky.

"And like I said, it's good evidence as long as it's authentic and came from where you claim it did," Officer Rhodes said. "But I only have your word on that. I can't prove it came from his house. And if he doesn't want to talk to me tonight, I'll have to see a judge. I can only go back and order Mr. Crowley to let me search his house and ask him questions if a judge says I can."

All the parents nodded like this wasn't crazy talk. Any reasonable grown-up would insist they break the door down and rescue the dogs. I bit my lip to stop myself from saying anything else.

"I'll give you an update after contacting Mr. Crowley," he said as he walked out the door, Barkley's collar looped over his wrist. Then he turned around, looking sternly at March and me. The porch light made the badge on his chest extra shiny and the shadows under his brow dark. "I don't know whether or not the collar will help us find Barkley or any of the other dogs," he said. "But it was dangerous to look through Mr. Crowley's garbage.

Do you understand? Whether or not he's a bad guy, you should never do any investigating—that's *our* job."

March nodded longer than necessary. I kept my head very still until Officer Rhodes turned around and walked back to his police car. Then I went back to the coffee table, grabbed the dog food receipt, and slipped it back into the pages of the Sleuth Chronicle.

CHAPTER TWENTY

March and his parents stayed until nine. That's when the grown-ups decided that perhaps Mr. Crowley wasn't even home for Officer Rhodes to question that night; we might not hear back for a while. The Winterses left, their arms limp at their sides, and my parents locked the house behind them. They latched the dead bolt and closed all the blinds while I watched from the window seat.

Dad called me into the kitchen, and I sat at the breakfast bar while Mom busied herself making tea.

"Kazu," he said, "we know you're worried about Barkley and the other missing dogs." Dad had bent over to rest his elbows on the countertop, making his eyes level with mine.

My parents were opposite in every way. Dad was tall, Mom was short. Dad athletic, Mom delicate. Dad jovial, Mom stern. Dad calm, Mom passionate. That's probably why Dad was usually assigned to talk to me when Mom felt too emotional. *Emotional* was code for spit angry, meaning she would yell with such force that spit would spray from her mouth like a mist. I could tell by the way Mom stood by the stove, waiting for the teapot to whistle, that she was pretty much there. Her shoulders were pushed back and her head held high as if holding it up prevented all the rage from boiling over.

"Even though you're worried, Bug," Dad said, reaching out to grab my hand, "you *cannot* try to solve these things." This time it was Dad who was stern, squeezing my hand a bit too tightly. Stern, but just like he always promised, cool as a cucumber.

"I wasn't trying to at first," I said. "But when I found the receipt in the recycled bags, I couldn't ignore it."

Mom spoke with the force of an arrow hitting a target. "You should've told us about the receipt." She folded her arms across her chest—a little high, like she was body-blocking her daughter's stupidity.

I knew I should keep quiet and not say another word, but I couldn't help myself. "You never would have listened to me," I said, my voice getting louder the more I spoke. "You treat me like a baby who doesn't know anything. It's like nothing I say or think matters."

Her face froze, a sheet of ice ready to crack. Dad stepped between us and flattened me with his eyes. "You and March cannot do that sort of thing again." Cool as a cucumber. "Do you understand me?"

I nodded. I had managed to get into trouble without an official grounding, and somehow that felt worse.

Mom set a cup of warm milk and honey in front of me, although she placed it with such force, some of the milk sloshed from the cup onto the counter. Sometimes, when I struggled to go to sleep, she would make it for me. "Drink this and go to bed," she ordered.

Mom ripped a paper towel from the dispenser and rubbed it between her hands. She dropped it into the trash can and left the room, not looking at me as she walked away.

I was almost asleep when I heard the doorbell ring. Mumbling voices echoed up from the entryway, and I tiptoed to my open door, where I could hear them more clearly. Officer Rhodes was telling my parents about Mr. Crowley's willingness to help them; apparently he had welcomed the police into his home, inviting them to perform a thorough search of his entire house.

"There was nothing there," Officer Rhodes said. "It would be impossible for him to hold any animals in that home. The basement is practically empty, and our team couldn't find a single trace of Barkley, or any dog, for that matter."

There was a long pause that neither of my parents tried to fill. Then Officer Rhodes continued. "Kazuko said she was the last to see Barkley, right?"

"That's correct." Dad used his work voice.

"Is it possible that Kazuko kept Barkley's collar after the dog disappeared?" A rush of heat rose to my face, and I felt dizzy like I had stood up too quickly. Officer Rhodes thought I was lying about finding Barkley's collar in Geezer's garbage can.

"Kazuko wouldn't do that," Dad said. "She may be nosy, but she's not hurtful or calculating—"

"No, no," Officer Rhodes interrupted him. "I wouldn't think that. But some kids around here are worked up over the dognappings. Maybe it was wishful thinking on her part. If Mr. Crowley was the bad guy and he got in trouble, then maybe she wouldn't feel so bad about losing Barkley."

Dad thanked Officer Rhodes but stated that it had been a long day for everyone. The officer wouldn't need to talk to me again; Dad assured him they would put an end to this business.

"But what we talked about tonight," Dad said, right before he said good-bye. "About Mr. Crowley and those things the kids found? That's on the record, right?"

"I'll make a report, and it will go in the file."

"That's good to know," Dad said, and the door creaked shut.

I listened as my parents locked up the main floor again. And even though my cheeks still burned from what Officer Rhodes had said about Barkley's dog collar, I could tell from Dad's voice that he believed me.

As I surrendered to the warmth of the sweet milk, I realized that Mom had said nothing the entire visit. And that was the loudest response of all.

CHAPTER TWENTY-ONE

The next day, I didn't talk at school. Not one word.

At first I didn't feel like it, but by lunch, it had become a challenge. It amazed me how many questions could be answered with simple gestures: nodding, shrugging, pointing. I had been wasting too much of my life talking, I decided.

March understood and probably didn't feel much like talking either. At recess, we sat on the swings and dragged our feet through the sand. CindeeRae found us and leaned against the swing set.

"Can we tell her?" March asked. He looked at me and raised his eyebrows.

I let out a heavy breath and nodded. Who cared

about our rules anymore? The operation was over. March explained everything to CindeeRae, her eyes widening with each new revelation.

"You know who the dognapper is?" she asked me when March had finished talking. Her voice always sounded like a television turned on full blast.

"Shhhhhhh." March looked around to make sure no one overheard. "Yes. We're pretty sure."

"What are we going to do?" For the first time since Lobster had disappeared, CindeeRae stood tall, like her spine had been fully inflated or something. "We should organize a search party, talk to reporters, go to the city council, contact the lead investigator on the case. Twenty dogs are missing, and one of them is Lobster. Something must be done!" I could almost see CindeeRae standing on stage, monologuing before a bright spotlight; she really was a natural.

March eyeballed her. "The police don't care." He paused as if waiting for her to jump in again. "The cop told us they have serious crimes to solve and can't be bothered by kids making trouble."

CindeeRae took the empty swing next to mine. "My aunt's a brand-new cop, and when Lobster disappeared they sent her over to take our report. I call her every day after school, and every day she says they're following lots of leads but haven't found the dognapper yet." She inhaled dramatically. "But *you* know who it is."

March shrugged. "It doesn't matter. Because of us, they think Mr. Crowley's clean."

"No way!" CindeeRae stood again, fist-hands at her side. "They have his information, and they won't forget. Plus, if he's the guy, all the clues will lead back to him. You need to follow up with that police officer."

"Officer Rhodes." March made a face when he said his name. "After he left, Dad said he looked like a bitter middle-aged Ron Weasley who abandoned wizardry for law enforcement."

I almost interrupted to remind him that Ron Weasley didn't have blond hair, but the idea of March's dad getting all spit angry about Officer Rhodes made me smile. I had worried that March's parents would believe the guy's story about Barkley's dog collar. But we weren't making it up; I knew Barkley, and probably Lobster, too, must have been at his house sometime. What else was he doing with all that dog food?

As if reading my mind, March said, "But they didn't find anything in his house."

"Not even one doggie treat?" CindeeRae asked. "Or a pile of dog poo?"

"I don't think they did any forensic testing," March said. "But no."

I nodded, kicking my feet together. Kids swarmed around the playground, weaving in and out of the jungle gym in front of the swings. A handful of third graders played tag on the monkey bars while two kids stared us down from atop the geodome.

CindeeRae took to her swing again, her voice dropping to a less theatrical volume. "The newspaper calls it a dognapping ring—that means lots of people, right? That means your paper-route guy's not the only one involved."

March nodded his head like CindeeRae was onto something. "You're right."

I dug my shoes into the sand and stopped the swing. Maybe Barkley, Lobster, and the other dogs Geezer took that day weren't even there by the time I found the receipt. Geezer's house was clean, and Officer Rhodes said there was no way any dogs had been kept there. Someone else *had* to be involved.

My voice croaked when I finally spoke. "Maybe it's Geezer's job to take them, but it's someone else's job to hold them."

They both stared at me, shocked that I had finally spoken.

March and I had thought Geezer was the boss of the Denver Dognapping Ring. But there had to be more people helping him out. And what if those people kept the dogs after Geezer swiped them, at least until they placed them with the illegal breeders and dogfighters? Because if they didn't hold on to the dogs for at least a little bit, they wouldn't need fifteen bags of dog food to feed them.

CindeeRae jumped out of her swing and scrambled to the space between March and me. She stood like a slingshot, pulled tight and ready to launch. "We've got to find out where they go!" Her cheeks reddened, matching her hair. She was practically beaming.

As CindeeRae bounced on her heels, March watched me, trying to read my expression. All our clues had been worthless so far, and the case was much more complicated than we had thought. How would we find out where they held the dogs?

"We need a new operation." I spoke my second and third full sentences of the day. "Locate Doggie-Holding Headquarters."

The three of us had decided to search Lakeview Park after school for more clues. March and I would ride the bus to his house, where I would borrow Mason's bike, and CindeeRae would meet us at the park on hers.

But Geezer was waiting when we got off the bus.

At first I thought he was an afternoon kindergartner's grandpa and turned toward March's house without a thought. But March froze at the base of the bus steps as kids flooded past him. After everyone had exited the bus, the driver pulled the lever for the door, and it closed with the sound of a monster's sigh. The bus drove away, and within seconds the three of us were standing together in the middle of March's block.

Mr. Crowley gestured to himself. "I'm James Crowley. March and I already know each other." He clapped a firm hand on March's shoulder. I had never seen Mr. Crowley in person before, and I didn't expect him to be so tall and fit. He didn't look much like a Geezer as he did an old model who owned a chain of fitness clubs and drank power shakes.

Then he extended his hand toward me for a shake. "Kazuko, I assume?" Without thinking, I shook his hand, and he squeezed back, hard.

"Look," he said. "I don't want there to be any hard feelings, okay?"

March and I nodded, and my hand throbbed for a bit even after he let it go. I looked to March's house, ready to grab his hand and sprint for the front door, but Mr. Crowley caught my gaze and took two steps forward to block our path.

"I understand that you kids are scared and would like to figure out who's taking all these dogs." He put his hands on his hips, making his shoulders look broader. His longish white hair was held back in a thin ponytail. "But I hope you realize now that I'm not your guy, right?"

Again we nodded, stiffly. My heart roared in my ears; I was sure March could hear it, too.

"The polite thing to do is answer when someone asks you a question," Mr. Crowley said. He bent at the waist to look in our eyes. His were gray like wet stones.

"You're not our guy," March whispered.

Mr. Crowley looked at me. "Kazuko?" he asked, his voice chirpy.

"We're sorry." My voice cracked. "We know it's not you," I lied.

"Well, good," he said, standing tall. "Now we can get to the business of being friends."

March smiled, but it was the twitchy look of a wild animal. I tugged on his arm and backed toward his house.

"Have a good night," Mr. Crowley said.

We ran away, the gravel kicking up around our feet as we went. "Be careful!" he called after us. "With all those dogs disappearing, you wouldn't want yours to be next."

I thought of Genki circling Jimmy Mason to protect me. But then I remembered all the times his social anxiety disorder left him cowering under the dining room table. Loud noises, strangers, the ruffling of aluminum foil all upset him. It took a while to coax him away from the table and up to my room, where I'd make a blanket nest and snuggle him to sleep. Imagining Genki in the back of Mr. Crowley's dirty dognapping van made my chest expand as if my lungs were on fire.

Crowley had stolen twenty dogs like Genki who were afraid and missing home. And twenty families wondered if they would ever see their dogs again. I wished the weight of all that sadness could trap Crowley like an avalanche.

"Listen, *friend*!" I had turned around and stood with my legs apart. "Your dognapping days are over."

Mr. Crowley turned around slowly, a half smile making his face look lopsided. And scary. Then he sauntered back toward his house, and I ran to catch up with March, my legs ready to buckle.

CHAPTER TWENTY-TWO

By late October the park cleared out except for serious joggers and dedicated dog walkers. March, CindeeRae, and I circled the loop on our bikes searching for clues and trying to come up with a new plan.

After telling her about our run-in with Crowley, no one had said much except CindeeRae, who had whispered, "This is like a real-life spy movie," only she didn't seem especially excited at the idea.

Crowley's threat had done the opposite of what he'd intended; instead of making me afraid, he had made me angry. We had already given our biggest piece of evidence to the police—Barkley's collar—and it hadn't helped. But there had to be more clues somewhere. Since we knew Crowley had taken Barkley from Lakeview, and since his house was just around the corner, we thought the park might be his favorite swiping spot. Hopefully he had left something behind on the road or even in the garbage cans that would help us figure out where he kept the dogs after he stole them. And if he hadn't, we'd have to figure out somewhere else we could find clues.

We couldn't just give up and let the bad guy win.

"This is a bad idea, Kazu." March's voice barely carried over the wind to where I led the group. "What if he's out prowling and sees us?"

"Unless you can uncover more evidence through your hack, we won't find anything by hiding inside," I called to him over my shoulder without looking back. Keeping my bike upright against the wind required all my concentration. "You really want to wait for Crowley to come after us? He's already got Lobster. You want him to take Genki and Hopper, too?"

"Better Hopper than me," I could have sworn I heard him mutter. But with the tree-bending wind and rush-hour traffic on Federal Boulevard, I couldn't be sure.

CindeeRae passed March and pedaled so that her bike was even with mine. "Maybe we should spy on him? Wait until he leaves his house and follow him to the scene of the next dognapping."

That actually wasn't a bad idea, but it probably wouldn't take him long to notice three kids trailing him on bikes—that is, if he didn't lose us in his dust first.

"Good suggestion," I yelled. "But let's try gathering more intel before we plan another high-stakes mission." After March's and my confession, followed by Officer Rhodes's visit to our house, Mom had barely talked to me. She would kill me if she found out I was trailing Crowley, and Crowley might kill us if *he* found out.

"Totally." CindeeRae stood on her pedals to push against the wind. "We can't go into a situation blind. We need information, lots more information . . ." A gust blew her words away.

The cold air bit at my ankles, which peeked from under my jeans as I rode. Socks were good for more than what Mom called stink-resistance, I decided. My windbreaker flapped and my eyes watered at the chill. I swerved toward a garbage can, stopped my bike, and peered over the rim to see if there was enough trash to rummage through. It was empty. We had picked a bad day to gather intel.

I shook my head at March and CindeeRae before standing on my pedals and powering forward; our parents wouldn't want us out riding past dinner. I ducked my head against the wind as we flew down the shady path behind Pioneer Village. We checked one more garbage can and a dumpster in the overflow parking lot. Nothing.

It was crazy to hope Crowley would leave behind evidence: a leash, a dog tag, another collar. Even an empty bag of doggie treats would be better than nothing.

It was crazier to hope he'd leave behind a map to the doggie-holding headquarters. We were going to have to look somewhere else for that.

As we rounded the corner and hit the long road beside the soccer field, we came upon a boy. He sat on the ground, leaning back against his elbows, the knees of his jeans ripped and bloody, an empty dog leash in his hand. His shoulders shook, and the movement rocked his whole body.

I stopped my bike so quickly it skidded on the path, shooting gravel from my back wheel. March and CindeeRae stopped behind me.

"Are you okay?" I leaned toward him over my bike.

The kid's eyes were glassy, and one tear slid down his cheek, clearing a path through the grime on his face. "He took my dog."

We had been here the entire time and had ridden round the loop twice. Were we so focused on finding clues that we had missed witnessing an actual dognapping?

The kid stood and started to jog toward Federal Boulevard. "I've got to go home and call the police."

We kept up with him on our bikes, riding slowly to match his pace. His hair was dark and wavy, and he wore a baseball tee with the number ten on the back. I thought I might have seen him at school. Was he a third grader?

"Is your name Dimitri?" CindeeRae asked. He nodded.

March and I turned to CindeeRae. Did she know *everyone* at Lincoln Elementary?

She shrugged. "My reading buddy was in his class last year."

Dimitri stopped, as if all our talking made him forget what he was doing. "A van stopped next to us, and this guy opened the door and took Muffin."

"What did he look like?" I grabbed the Sleuth Chronicle from my basket and opened it to a clean sheet of paper.

Dimitri looked around like he suddenly realized he was lost. He spun a slow circle, and the leash, missing its snap hook, flew in the wind like an empty kite string. I pictured myself down at the other end of the soccer field days ago with an empty leash in my own hand.

"I don't know," Dimitri said, meeting my eyes for the first time. "He was wearing a mask."

"Was someone with him?" My pen bled into the paper as I waited.

"No." He turned around and began walking toward Summer Glen. A slow hiccuping cry started from deep in his throat. "I wouldn't let go, so he cut the leash with a knife and drove away."

I wrote madly. "Which way did he go?"

"That way." He pointed over his shoulder toward Federal Boulevard.

"What did the van look like?"

"Big? No windows on the side, and pictures with writing that I couldn't really read. It was too dirty."

I tapped my pen on the notebook. It had to be the same van!

"We'll take you home." March slid from his bike and walked it to the other side of Dimitri so that we flanked him like guards. Dimitri's shoulders quaked with sobs.

Aside from me staring down the dognapping van after Crowley took Barkley, no one had seen the dognapper in action until today. Dimitri's dog must have been special.

"What kind of dog was Muffin?" I asked.

"A Samoyed puppy."

I had no idea what a Samoyed looked like, but I guessed they were expensive, or else why would Crowley risk snatching Muffin in broad daylight while Dimitri held fast to his leash? Muffin might go for a nice sum to an illegal breeder or a puppy mill, and Crowley obviously didn't care who else he might hurt in the process, as long as he got the dog.

We shadowed Dimitri to his house on Grove Street, where his mother pulled him into a tight hug before rushing down their front steps and hugging us, too. We hadn't seen anything, so we didn't have much to say, but we nodded dumbly as we listened to Dimitri choke out something in Spanish, his words catching in his throat with his tears.

As March, CindeeRae, and I walked our bikes four blocks to my house, I realized that, with all the details of Muffin's dognapping tucked neatly inside the pages of the Sleuth Chronicle, we had only discovered one thing: Crowley was even more dangerous than we'd first thought.

CHAPTER TWENTY-THREE

The lunchroom sounded like a gaggle of geese during the week before Halloween. The tables were already crowded by the time we walked in, and the place smelled like spaghetti sauce and sour milk. March and I sat in the back corner with CindeeRae, Pat, and Jared.

Jared placed a bag of Flamin' Hot Cheetos in the middle of the table for trade, and I snatched them, dropping a bag of grapes in their place. CindeeRae pushed a sandwich bag full of graham crackers next to them and said, "Is anyone even going trick-or-treating? Since Lobster . . ." She fiddled with her juice box. "The Denver Dognapper freaks my parents out, and they won't let me."

"I think so," Pat said, and Jared nodded.

I looked at March. We had been going trick-or-treating together for years, but after getting in trouble for Mission: Geezer's Garbage Raid, we hadn't talked about it. I shrugged, and March said, "This is my last eligible year for T-or-T. Someone will pay if I can't go."

T-or-T was what March called trick-or-treating. I had never heard anyone else call it that, including his family.

"I'm glad my parents don't want me to go," CindeeRae said, but even with all her acting skills, I didn't believe her.

"But your parents could always go with you." March pushed a single yellow Starburst to the center of the table with his pointer finger.

"Or you could go with us?" I snatched the Starburst, without offering anything else for trade. March scowled at me, and I said, "It's *one* Starburst. It shouldn't even count as anything."

"What do you think of a party instead?" CindeeRae had gotten better about turning down her voice, but she was still the loudest one at the table. "We could eat lots of junk food without having to work for it."

Jared and Pat nodded, considering. I almost nodded with them before realizing March would think I was a huge traitor for even thinking about it, so I ducked my head instead. That's when I caught sight of Madeleine Brown passing our table and shushed everyone. She stopped at the sound and turned toward us, eyebrows tilting together like they were conspiring.

"You babies want to go trick-or-treating?" She plopped down next to March with Catelyn. "I mean, aren't fifth graders too old to go trick-or-treating?" Madeleine wore a T-shirt with the number fourteen on the front.

"T-or-T is cool," March said, and I cringed. Didn't he know this was the worst possible moment to use his weird Halloween lingo? "Dressing up is fun, and you get *free* candy. What fifth grader doesn't like free candy?"

"*T-or-T is cool,*" she mimicked, rolling her eyes. I stayed silent. Madeleine leaned across the table toward me. "What are *you* going to be for Halloween, Detective Jones? A superhero crime fighter? Sherlock Holmes?"

My chocolate milk begged me to pour it over her head—the carton nearly twitched in my hand. I took a deep breath instead—even though the thought of Madeleine Brown walking home with sour-milk hair made me smile.

"What's so funny?" she asked. "Is that what detectives do when someone asks them a hard question?"

She made detecting sound silly, babyish even. I leaned across the table and said, "Would you like it if I made fun of you for dressing up with a bunch of people in matching uniforms to chase a ball around? Probably not, because it's mean. You can make anything sound dumb if you try hard enough. It's sad that you want to be good at that."

Catelyn's eyebrows shot up. Madeleine's face was all pinched, like someone had cranked her nose a couple times.

Madeleine stood and slammed her palms on the tabletop. "You, and all your friends, are *freaks*!" She stomped off, Catelyn shuffling behind to keep up.

We sat quietly for a few seconds. Then March said, "That was the coolest thing *ever*." He pushed three more Starbursts to me across the table.

"Totally!" CindeeRae said, and we all hooted together, celebrating.

CHAPTER TWENTY-FOUR

By the time I got home from school, I was over our cafeteria victory and angry that Madeleine Brown had made fun of me and my detecting. Just thinking about it sent a stinging flush to my cheeks.

I slammed our front door behind me.

Genki heard and ran down the stairs. But then he read my mood and lay down by my feet, licking the bare skin at my ankles.

From where I stood I could see Mom at the kitchen counter making baked manicotti. In one hand she held a pasta shell and in the other a plastic bag full of the cheese filling. Two long rows of the stuffed shells lined the casserole dish at her side. I breathed in the happy scent, and exhaled a bit of anger. Baked manicotti was my favorite.

Pearl Jam blasted from the portable speakers on the counter, Mom's third-favorite band behind the Smashing Pumpkins and the Red Hot Chili Peppers. She probably didn't even hear the door slam.

"What's wrong?" Mom asked, squeezing the mixture into the last shell. She wedged it into the casserole dish and looked at me.

When I didn't answer, she wiped her hands on the towel hung over her shoulder and turned off the music.

The silence swallowed the room. "Today stunk!" I said.

She walked toward me, a big smile stretching her cheeks. "I may have something that will make you feel better."

I was ready to list everything about the day that had upset me, my complaints about Madeleine Brown stacked on my tongue. Without anywhere to go, I swallowed them down, and it left my chest tight and hot.

Mom pointed to the window seat before turning back to her chore. Laid out on the navy cushions was a Velma costume, complete with an oversize orange turtleneck, a red skirt, orange knee-highs, and red Mary Janes. It was perfect and horrible at the same time.

"I don't want to be Velma anymore," I whispered.

Mom froze. "Why not?" The smile had completely melted from her face. But my cheeks still burned as I remembered Madeleine's sneer.

"Because it's stupid," I blurted. "It's a baby costume." Everything I said was wrong, but I meant it. I was surprised those two things could happen at the same time.

Mom didn't reply, but got back to work covering the manicotti with marinara sauce, her eyes down. I felt silly, stranded in the entryway to our house with my backpack still on my shoulders.

As I slipped off my shoes and turned toward the stairway, Mom spun around, her face red. *"Shitsurei!" How rude.* She leaned forward on the counter, palms down. The pose made her look big and angry. Spit angry.

"I give up, Kazuko!" Her lips trembled as she spoke. "You're constantly getting into trouble, and you never want to spend time with your family anymore! And when I go out of my way to get you something you asked for less than a week ago, you tell me it's stupid."

Genki whimpered at my feet and then walked toward the dining room, where he would probably quiver under the table for about forty minutes.

"Go to your room. I don't want to see you before dinner."

I felt anchored to the floor, shocked by Mom's response.

"Did you hear me?" she asked.

Genki whined from the other room, as if he were answering for me.

"Yes, Mom." And as respectfully as possible, I shifted my eyes away and walked upstairs to my room, careful to close the door quietly behind me.

Dad came into my room after he got home from work, holding a pink plastic brain in one hand. "Hey, Bug." He walked to my bed and sat next to me, squeezing the squeaky brain before dropping it next to me on the floor. His green button-down shirt was crisp and smelled like a forest cologne. As soon as he smiled, my heart didn't feel so heavy.

"Wow! Your room's looking nice."

I gathered all my homework and pushed it into its folder. For two hours I had cleaned my room and then decided I should probably catch up on spelling assignments. "Mom's kinda mad at me, so I thought I should do something she'd like."

"Yeah. I heard you had a scuffle this afternoon. Mom's stress about the exhibit, and this whole dognapping business, is taking its toll. On both of you."

"Maybe." I slid the folder into my backpack and

scooted closer to Dad. He pulled me to his side and draped his arm around my shoulder. I closed my eyes and leaned into him, inhaling his scent.

"I think we all need to do something fun," Dad said. "What do you think about heading to Sleepy Hollow as soon as it gets dark?"

Sleepy Hollow was an actual street in Highlands Prime—a rich Denver suburb—and every Halloween the houses were decorated with elaborate lights and displays. The week before the thirty-first they had a big block party every night where vendors set up food trucks and picture booths or sold glow-in-the-dark trinkets and face painting. People in crazy costumes wove down the street, and many residents staged events in their front yards, like a witch's brew with hags bent over a smoking cauldron or a mini–spook alley weaving through a make-shift maze.

There was even a doggie parade, where owners walked their costumed pets up and down the block. This wasn't Genki's favorite activity, since he was prone to public panic attacks, but when we picked the right costume—mostly cloaky ones that hid his face—he did okay. Two years ago he even placed in the Puppy Dog Masquerade, although someone entered their cat and Genki disqualified himself by chasing it through the neighborhood. March and I spent the entire night running after him, Genki's Little Red Riding Hood costume catching air like a parachute.

I almost liked going to Sleepy Hollow more than I liked trick-or-treating, except there wasn't as much candy.

"I really don't feel like it," I said.

"Come on, Kazu. We haven't missed a night at Sleepy Hollow for ten years now. We're not starting this Halloween."

I nodded because I couldn't think of another response.

"Let's go and have a good time, all decked out." He leaned over and grabbed the pink brain before handing it to me.

"Do you think Mom will still let me wear the Velma costume?" I ducked my head so I wouldn't have to look in his eyes.

He bent toward me and whispered, "I heard you said it was too babyish."

I looked at Dad, hoping he could see all that I hadn't been able to tell Mom that afternoon. "Maybe for school. But not for Sleepy Hollow or trick-or-treating." Not for times when Madeleine Brown couldn't see me.

Dad nodded like what I said made sense. After a pause he asked, "Why didn't you tell Mom that, Bug?"

I could only shrug. For some reason, Mom triggered my most honest reactions minus the charm or courtesy reserved for other adults. It's like I couldn't help myself when she was around; it spewed out unchecked, like foam from a shaken soda bottle.

"Grab your Velma costume and get ready." Dad stood and walked toward the door. "March is coming with us, so be prepared to party hard with Steve Jobs."

Even at my glummest, I had to smile at that. "Is it okay if we invite one more person?" I asked.

He was already thudding down the stairs when he yelled his response. "Of course!"

Dad ducked his head to fit in the car, and the black tips of his Dragon Ball Z wig bent against the car's ceiling. Mom smoothed down her costume after clicking the seat belt in place. She didn't care that the real Wonder Woman hadn't worn blue pleather leggings and a red, white, and blue cape; she claimed her makeshift costume kept her warm.

"You ready for this, Kazu?" she asked like we were going to the doctor's. We hadn't officially made up yet, but going to Sleepy Hollow together seemed an unspoken truce. It helped that I wore the Velma costume. Plus, I cleaned my room, so I had practically apologized out loud.

"Yes," I said. "But we don't have to stay for very long."

"Are you kidding?" Dad said. "I look forward to this all year." He turned to smile at me, and the motion nearly pulled the plastic wig from his head. He yanked it down before turning back in his seat, and it snapped against his neck like a rubber band.

I yanked the seat belt over my orange turtleneck sweater, poking Genki, who was trying to snuggle my side.

"Genki's hot-dog costume is cool," I said, petting the mustard stripe down his back.

"It just accentuates what we already knew." Dad started the car and pulled from the driveway, the sky darkening quickly as the sun went down. Turning onto March's street made me antsy, and when Dad told me to run and grab March, I asked him to honk the horn instead. I knew Mr. Crowley wouldn't terrorize me in front of my parents, but I didn't want to risk meeting him on the street again.

March's mom walked him to the car and then leaned in to chat with Mom as March climbed into the backseat.

"Steve Jobs won?" I asked.

He was wearing a long-sleeved black turtleneck shirt with a white apple on the chest, jeans, and tennis shoes. His mom had buzzed his hair, and he wore wire-frame Gandhi glasses.

"It wasn't much of a contest."

"Are you going to carry that the whole time?" I asked him.

March held a white iPhone box in one hand—his prop.

"Are you going to carry *that* the whole time?" He motioned at the Sleuth Chronicle clutched to my chest.

"Yes." I couldn't think of a better Velma accessory.

March shrugged. "I can put the box in my back pocket if I need to." He leaned forward to get a better look at me. "Nice seventies costume."

"Velma!" I said. "You know, from *Scooby-Doo.*"

He gave me a slow nod and then said, "Sheesh, you're grouchy."

We both sat back in the seat and looked out opposite windows. As Dad turned from Colonial to Summer Glen, we passed Mr. Crowley's house.

A chill traveled my spine, and I looked away.

CHAPTER TWENTY-FIVE

The closer it got to Halloween, the more crowded Sleepy Hollow became. The blocked-off street was flooded with small families and their toddling children. March, CindeeRae, and I stopped to take it all in. Dad had picked up CindeeRae on the way, and she wore a black hoodie with ears, a furry white bib, and matching leg warmers over black leggings and ballet shoes.

As she twirled ahead of me, a kitty tail flared out behind her. "You're a cat?" I asked in a hushed voice, afraid Mom might overhear and want to trade me in for CindeeRae, a kid willingly dressing up as a cat for Halloween.

"Not just *any* cat," CindeeRae said. "Mr. Mistoffelees."

"What?" I asked.

"It's from my very favorite Broadway musical, *Cats*." She twitched her kitty nose and did some bouncy ballet moves.

"You guys coming?" Mom called over her shoulder as Dad pulled her toward our favorite food truck. We hustled after them. March and I taught CindeeRae how to play slug-bug Halloween, yelling out duplicates as we saw them: three Spider-Mans, two Captain Americas, three pumpkins, four skeletons, two zombie cheerleaders, another Goku from Dragon Ball Z.

We each grabbed an order of mummy dogs with purple and orange Halloween fries, which were really made from two different kinds of sweet potatoes. We ate at a nearby picnic table and strained our necks to see where we wanted to go first. March called the bounce house at the end of the street, while I argued for the haystack maze two houses down; CindeeRae seconded my motion. I liked having her around.

A big group crowded around the food truck. "Let's get out of here before that family of Incredibles takes us out," Dad said.

As we made our way toward the Pumpkin House, covered in orange lights with a lawn full of jack-o'-lanterns, we bumped into Mrs. Hewitt—well, actually Mom did. She slammed into her hard enough to knock the golden lasso from her utility belt. Mrs. Hewitt took the blow, sturdy as a tree stump.

"My Lincoln Elementary Singers!" she cried, holding her arms straight out like she meant to hug us. She wore a red wig and bright red lipstick that bled into the lines around her mouth. A white apron cinched her waist and her tights bagged at her ankles, above heavy black shoes with Velcro.

"I'm sorry," Mom said, reaching out to steady her. "Mrs. Hewitt, right? District music teacher?" I began to fidget, worrying that Mrs. Hewitt might rat me out for pegging her in the face with a Jolly Rancher, or worse yet, tell Mom I was practicing the duet with Madeleine Brown as punishment for it.

Mrs. Hewitt nodded like Mom was asking if she were a movie star.

"You look great," Mom said. "We are huge *I Love Lucy* fans."

We were; I had watched all six seasons last summer, which we had gotten in a boxed set from my grandma on Dad's side. Even so, I couldn't tell who Mrs. Hewitt was dressed as until Mom said so.

"You all look grand as well," she said, and winked at me.

"Do you live here?" Dad asked Mrs. Hewitt.

"Oh, no," she said. "I come every night so Pickles can

walk the parade." I hadn't noticed the wiener dog sitting a couple feet away wearing a pickle costume.

I shifted my weight from one foot to the other.

"That's interesting," Mom said, which was really a polite way to say *weird*. They said good-bye, and March, CindeeRae, Genki, and I continued walking toward the haystack maze.

I caught a glimpse of Madeleine Brown skipping from the witch's brew to the little stand with a doughnut drop. She was dressed as a pirate and held pirate-twin Catelyn Monsen's hand. In the other hand she held a leash connected to a collie wearing red-and-white-striped leg warmers and a matching headscarf, the ears poking through the folds.

They skidded to a stop at the end of the line, Madeleine's and Catelyn's hands swinging between them. I paused, and March and CindeeRae walked on without me.

I stared at Madeleine as she leaned toward her dog to coo and scratch at his ears. And then I remembered her friend list:

- follows me
- sits on my feet
- plays soccer
- licks my tears

Madeleine Brown was being serious. Her best friend was her dog.

When CindeeRae noticed that I wasn't catching up, she grabbed March's arm and yelled back to me, "What are you waiting for?"

I put my finger on my lips to shush her and then pointed at Madeleine and Catelyn.

CindeeRae spotted them and laughed, her evil cackle echoing down the block. "Look who's a baby now, dressing up as a pirate for Halloween."

I shushed them.

Genki pulled at the leash, and I smiled. My list had been about March, but I could just as easily have made a list about my puppy.

Knowing her secret made the embarrassment from lunch disappear. A warmth spread through my chest. As if he understood, Genki looked up and panted at me, his mouth wide like he was grinning.

"Hurry up, Kazu." March waved me toward them, standing at the back of the haystack line. Genki and I ran to catch up.

We sat at a picnic table waiting for the puppy parade while eating "poisoned candy apples"; they were covered in a shiny black glaze that tasted like cotton candy. Mom and Dad had run into some friends and were drinking cider together one table down.

"What's next?" CindeeRae asked.

On the far end of Sleepy Hollow, a man dressed like a circus ringmaster motioned for the crowd of costumed dogs and their humans to form a single line. Genki lay at my feet, pooped from a long night of peopling.

"We need more clues," I said, rubbing his belly with my foot.

"We've looked everywhere," March said. "What else can we do?"

The ringmaster blew his whistle and motioned the parade forward. "The Monster Mash" blared from one of the Sleepy Hollow houses as dogs and people began the slow march through the neighborhood.

"The hack," I said, barely able to hear the words myself. This time when I spoke, my voice squeaked. "We didn't know what we were looking for before, but Crowley's got to communicate with his partners somehow. We need to check his e-mail again."

March and CindeeRae sat up taller. Hearing the excitement in my voice, Genki stood and dug his snout into my side, whining, and I couldn't tell if it was because he was worried about me or wanted help taking off his hot-dog costume.

The front of the parade drew closer, and smack-dab in the middle, Madeleine Brown and Catelyn Monsen walked their pirate dog. Behind them Mrs. Hewitt pranced next to Pickles.

"Let's check the hack tomorrow," CindeeRae said. "After school?"

"Tomorrow, after school," I agreed.

CHAPTER TWENTY-SIX

Madeleine Brown and Catelyn Monsen ducked behind the book-fair display in the library, their faces drawn. March and I side-eyed each other before sneaking around a spooky-book tower to listen in on their conversation.

Students who were up-to-date in the fifth-grade genre challenge filled the library. Eavesdropping in a small space filled with chatter tested our keenest spy skills. But we were real professionals, and March got to work blocking the noisiest of kids away from our target.

He grabbed a book in one hand, splayed its pages, and held it open with a thumb, moving back and forth behind me as if enthralled with the story. He mumbled apologies as he pushed into kids, like a human bumper car, clearing a quiet perimeter around Madeleine's hiding place. I leaned into the book display and strained to hear her and Catelyn talking.

There were whispers and . . . crying? Catelyn mumbled, "It's okay, they'll find him," while it sounded like Madeleine was weeping. I turned to meet March's eyes, raising my brows in confusion. I couldn't even picture Madeleine Brown crying. I spun back and leaned closer to hear her sputter, "We've had Lenny since he was a puppy. Now I may never see him again."

I backed away from the Halloween book display, a cramp pinching my side. Grabbing March's arm, I whispered, "I think Crowley stole Madeleine's dog."

We were halfway to our reading classes before we realized March had taken the library book without checking it out.

Hating Madeleine Brown wasn't nearly as fun now that she was sad. She stood in the middle of the choral risers wearing dark jeans and a black sweater. Her face was splotchy, like she had a rash, and her hair hung past her shoulders in stringy strands. Her friends, usually bouncing and giggling around her, watched her from the corners of their eyes.

Mrs. Hewitt was preparing us for the Halloween

assembly, where each class performed two songs. The fifth grade would sing "Ten Little Witches" and "Gory Monsters Galore," which ended with a chorus sure to inspire a handful of nightmares:

> *The gory monsters roam the street,*
> *Looking for a simple treat.*
> *Trickers, oh, look mighty tasty.*
> *Run like lightning, super hasty.*

The song was just missing a line about ogres picking their teeth with children's bones. Even so, I caught myself wishing Denver's monsters were purple cyclopes or slobbery beasts. Mr. Crowley was the worst kind of scary; he was real.

Mrs. Hewitt showed everyone how to sing from their diaphragms, pushing at a spot below her chest and singing words that began with HA. *HAppy HAndy HAmmer HAnky HA HA HA!* She reminded me of a teddy bear with a sound box hidden in the stuffing, the kind that you had to push on just right to make the plush laugh or sing or growl.

March towered above everyone on the top row, three up from Madeleine. He was serious about singing, and I could hear his tenor voice clearly, like he was exaggerating for a laugh. When I tried sending him a warning look,

he flashed me our secret hand signal—Taco Monster—
and kept singing.

Madeleine looked at him over her shoulder, but her
face remained expressionless. Any other time, March
would have been the target of a verbal Madeleine dart,
and her friends would have erupted in laughter. But
something about the way she turned back to face the
front of the class, her eyes flat and dark like buttons,
made me feel sorry for her.

Mrs. Hewitt now pantomimed the signs that went
with each line of the song. She used clawed fingers when
singing about monsters, a hand visor when searching for
treats, a tummy drum for tasty "trickers," and then the
running man on the final line warning everyone to flee.

"Creepy, right?" she asked the class after she finished,
breathing heavily from the effort.

She stood before the class, her arms held forward
like a zombie's. Maybe more strange than creepy, but it
worked for her.

After music class, as we walked up the stairs,
Madeleine caught up to me and grabbed my arm; her
fingernails dug into my skin. She whispered in my ear,
and her breath was hot. "You know who the Denver
Dognapper is. If you don't let me in on it, I'm going to
tell the police."

My ear felt wet, and I tried to wipe it dry with my

shoulder. "The joke's on you," I said. "We already told them, and they don't care."

She stopped walking, and for a minute I thought she would drop to the floor in a tantrum. Instead she marched forward, her face hardening to stone. "I need to get Lenny back. You have to tell me what you know."

Rule #2: Do not share operation intel with anyone else. But we had broken that rule when we told CindeeRae that we suspected Crowley was the dognapper, and she probably blabbed about it with her stage voice so that Madeleine finally overheard.

"We have some information," I admitted. I couldn't even hear my own whisper over the hallway chatter. "When we know more, we'll tell you."

As soon as I said the words, my limbs felt heavy.

Madeleine stopped at the bulletin board outside Mr. Carter's class. "I want in. *Now.*" Her eyes flashed, but for a moment I caught a glint of despair. I remembered her best friend list, and I imagined Madeleine's pirate puppy licking her tears, sitting on her feet, and following her to the soccer field.

"*Please?*" she added.

March and CindeeRae were going to kill me.

"Did you hear?" CindeeRae plopped into the seat across from March and me at the back of the school bus. She had given our driver a permission slip to ride with us to March's stop so we could search the back for more clues.

"You mean about Madeleine's dog being swiped from Sleepy Hollow last night?" I said, realizing that if March and CindeeRae felt bad enough for Madeleine, they might not be angry at me for inviting her to help us.

"She cried through most of social studies," March said.

I frowned at that information, trying to build sympathy for our nemesis.

"It makes me hate her less," CindeeRae said, gazing out the back window as the bus pulled from the turnout. "Maybe Lobster and her dog are friends now. Wouldn't that be weird?"

"Lenny," I said.

"What?" March asked.

"Lenny," I said again as March and CindeeRae studied me. "Her dog's name is Lenny."

"Look!" March pointed out the window as we passed the front of the school, and CindeeRae crowded next to us to get a peek.

Madeleine and Catelyn were walking toward the pickup lane, Madeleine wilting with each step, as if standing upright all day had finally taken its toll. Madeleine's mom waved the two girls toward her, and when Madeleine reached the car she collapsed into her mom's arms. I couldn't tell from where we sat, but I imagined her mom's eyes were red-rimmed like CindeeRae's mom's had been a couple weeks ago. Do all moms give their kids rides home from school when their pets have been dognapped?

"That's horrible." CindeeRae backed into her own seat and deflated into the cushion. "I remember that feeling." She shook her head like she was trying to dislodge the memory from her brain.

Now was the perfect time to break the news. "Speaking of horrible things," I said. "Madeleine somehow kinda heard that we know who the Denver Dognapper is."

"She what?!" March's voice was shrill, pinging off the walls of the school bus.

"I know, right?" I folded my arms over my chest, annoyed. "How did that even happen?" I looked from March to CindeeRae, letting my gaze linger on the newest member of our team.

CindeeRae twisted her fingers on her lap. "I was defending *you*, Kazu."

"Defending me from what?"

CindeeRae jutted out her lower lip and sighed, the force blowing up her curly red bangs. "Madeleine and Catelyn were making fun of *Detective Jones* in science class a couple days ago, and I couldn't let them say that stuff about you."

"What did you say?" March leaned forward in his seat so he could drill CindeeRae with his squinty eyes.

"Just that Kazu's already figured out who the Denver Dognapper is." She shrugged. "They didn't even believe me—they laughed and called me Little Watson."

"Now that she knows," I said, as if everything that happened next was out of my control, "she's forced herself into the group. Her mom's dropping her off at March's this afternoon."

"What?" March squealed again, this time his voice shriller than before. "Kazuko Jones, what are you talking about?"

"She was sad, guys." I tapped my foot on the floor, staring at the green backrest of the seat in front of us. "Maybe she can help."

"Help make the dognapper cry?" CindeeRae shifted in her seat to display perfect, board-straight posture. "Because the only thing that girl is good at is being mean."

"She's going to help us solve the case," I said, feeling for the first time like my detecting hobby had become a little too complicated, even for me. "It's going to be fine."

Even though March and CindeeRae didn't respond, their matching glares told me they didn't agree.

CHAPTER TWENTY-SEVEN

CindeeRae, Madeleine, and I hovered above March at his computer. Even Madeleine's swollen eyes hadn't done much to persuade March and CindeeRae that she would make a good member of our team. And when the first thing Madeleine did was make a crack about March's space-themed room being the perfect place for a spacey kid, any sympathy we might have had soured on the spot.

We watched March use his smarty-pants hacking skills to run a bunch of e-mail searches, finding nothing. He changed tactics and started looking for e-mails sent on the date of each dognapping, with me using the Sleuth Chronicle to guide him through the timeline.

When a search on Lenny's snatch date returned

nothing, Madeleine barked, "Did you search for 'dognapping'?" It sounded more like a command than a question.

"Anything with the word *dog* would have shown up when I ran that search," March said. "Like, forever ago."

"Plus." CindeeRae's voice was sharp and theater-loud again. "The dognapper would be pretty stupid to use those words if he was trying not to get caught."

Madeleine stepped back and rolled her eyes.

CindeeRae was right. Crowley was smarter than we thought; he covered his tracks, even in his in-box.

"How about something like *transport* or *delivery*?" CindeeRae's voice had quieted as she focused on sleuthing. She was a natural at detecting. "He must be replacing the word *dog* with something else, but he'd still need to schedule times to meet with people and make deliveries."

"Good," I said, catching her eye and smiling.

March punched at his keyboard, running a series of searches without finding anything suspicious.

Madeleine pulled away from the group and dropped into March's rocket beanbag, which he'd had since kindergarten. She hit the bag with such force, I expected tiny white balls to shoot from the stitching. It wasn't a big-kid beanbag. "Maybe they call each other instead. You know, because it leaves less evidence."

March's fingers froze over the keyboard, and the flutter of excitement in my chest turned to an anxious quiver. Madeleine had a point; the Denver Dognapping

Ring might be avoiding e-mail because it left a trail. If there was still no evidence from March's hack, where else could we search for information on the doggie-holding headquarters?

The four of us exchanged looks, and I said, "Keep running your searches, March. CindeeRae, Madeleine, and I will review all our evidence to see if we missed something."

I grabbed March's Christmas safe from his desk and had CindeeRae and Madeleine turn around while I pulled the key from beneath the mattress on the top bunk of March's bed. Giving them the okay, I opened the safe and spread all the contents on the floor. Printouts of Crowley's internet bookmarks, order history, web cache, and bank account information were fanned out on the rug. From the Sleuth Chronicle I pulled all the newspaper articles and the dog food receipt, adding them to the display. After a pause, I set the open notebook, with all my case notes, on the floor as well. CindeeRae and I stood back and eyed the evidence.

Madeleine let out a big huff. "This is stupid. We're not going to find anything standing around like this."

CindeeRae shushed her, and I said, "All good detectives have to research before they catch the bad guys."

Madeleine didn't argue, and we studied the information for a bit longer, our heads cocking back and forth. CindeeRae bent over and picked up the receipt. She held it close to her face and then far away as she ogled it. "It looks like someone wrote on this."

Madeleine snatched it from CindeeRae's fingers, studying the receipt with one eye closed. "She's right. There's handwriting on it, but someone's erased it or something."

March had stopped typing to watch us.

"I don't think anyone wrote on it," I said, "at least not on the receipt." I walked over to March and reached around him to rummage through his top desk drawer. Grabbing a pencil and a scrap of paper, I walked back to where Madeleine stood holding the receipt. "Someone probably wrote something down on another piece of paper that was on top of the receipt, and it left an indentation."

I took the receipt and walked back to the desk, laid it under a scrap of paper, and scribbled on top with the long edge of a pencil lead. I turned it so they could all see; the pencil had shaded everything except the writing on the receipt, which looked like it was in another language.

"Turn the receipt around," CindeeRae said. "It's backward."

I turned the receipt upside down, covered it with the blank corner of scrap paper, and shaded it again with the pencil. They had moved to the desk, where they hovered around me as I worked, two words slowly appearing on the edge of the receipt:

I dropped the pencil onto March's desktop while he leaped from his seat to do a victory dance, which looked a lot like the Funky Chicken.

CindeeRae eyed him. "It's just a street name, not a full address. And is there even a Dickinson Street in Denver?"

"Let's see." March's arms stopped flapping and he slid back into his desk chair and pulled up a mapping application on his computer screen. As he typed in the street name, we all leaned over him like we were about to discover the secret of the universe.

Someone barged into the room and slammed the door against the doorstep, the spring thwanging. We jumped.

Mason stood at the base of the bunk bed, frozen. "Hi," he said, his hands fidgeting in front of him while he slowly backed toward the door. He held a thin red rope that pooled at his feet. "I didn't know . . . everyone was here."

My heart pattered in my chest, and CindeeRae bent over like she had just finished a marathon.

"Get out, Mase," March snapped. "We're busy."

"Sheesh, March," I said. "Hey, Mason, it's no big deal."

"Hey, Kazu," he said, before zipping out the door and slamming it.

Madeleine crowded behind us to look at the computer screen, and I imagined a dark shadow falling over us all as she did.

"Well?" She talked to March like he was a waiter late with her food. "Is there a Dickinson Street in Denver?"

March tossed a glare over his shoulder at Madeleine before pointing at his screen. "Yep. There it is."

A thick yellow line seemed to split the entire map of Denver in two.

"What are we waiting for?" Madeleine asked. "Let's go."

"Go where?" I said. "Do you see how long that street is? Without an address, we have nothing."

Madeleine sighed with such force, it sounded more like a growl. "You guys aren't very good at this."

"Look," I said. "Searching for clues sometimes takes a lot of time. And if you don't have the patience, you should probably leave now."

"Yeah!" CindeeRae added.

We stood there as the awkward silence settled over us.

Madeleine's voice cut through the quiet, only it was softer, almost apologetic. "What do we do next?"

I nodded, thinking. "Let's divide up the clues and study them tonight." I gathered the papers into a stack so March could take them to his mom's office and make copies. "Maybe one of us will see something new."

CHAPTER TWENTY-EIGHT

had laid the copies out on my bedroom floor, picking up each piece and studying it upside down, hoping to uncover a case-cracking clue. Genki sat at attention by my door, as if on lookout, although he probably just needed to pee. I ignored him while I moved from one piece of information to the next.

When I got to the receipt, Mom burst into my bedroom, and Genki dashed through the open door.

"Could you please put the dishes away?" she asked, looking from me to the floor. She took one large step to tower over my work, scooped up a handful of papers, and shuffled through them, the crease between her eyebrows deepening with each sheet. I was pretty sure she had already forgotten about the dishes. "What is this?" She shook the stack of papers at me.

"My notes on the case," I said.

"Do you realize how dangerous this is?" Even though it was a question, I knew better than to answer. "Your father and I told you to stop this, this snooping. A policeman told you to stop snooping. But here you are . . . snooping!"

Luckily March and CindeeRae were reviewing the printouts from the hack, which left me and Madeleine with newspaper articles, Sleuth Chronicle notes, and the Crowley information I had found online. Still, Mom was not happy about it. I tried to stay calm and think through my response so that she could understand why detecting meant so much to me. But her face, twisted in disappointment, seemed to draw out all my emotions.

"I think this is important. You wouldn't be mad about it if you thought it was important, too," I said. "If you even tried to understand you would see that I want to find the dogs so they can go home."

"You're only eleven." She mumbled more to herself than me. "What are you thinking?"

As if she were saving the printouts from a gust of wind, Mom scrambled to pick up the rest, snatching the Sleuth Chronicle last. She hastily shoved the loose sheets into the middle of the journal. "You are done with this."

Her voice was even, her eyes hardening. "If I see or hear one more word about *investigating* or *detecting*, you might never see the sun again."

Even I could tell when parents exaggerated to make a point, but in that moment, I believed her. Snatching the receipt from my hand, she turned on her heels and marched out the door, slamming it behind her before Genki had a chance to slip back into my room.

March, CindeeRae, and I huddled on one of the benches lining the playground while Madeleine stood to the side, trying to edge closer to the group. Everyone held a file of clues, except me.

"You're grounded?" CindeeRae asked.

"Kinda?" It shouldn't have been a question, but it still came out as one. "From investigating?" I couldn't help it.

"I don't like this, Kazu," March said. "Your mom has never taken away your Sleuth Chronicle before."

I slumped against the bench, my lower back pushing into the wood. "I know. She's really mad at me."

"So that's it?" Madeleine waved her folder like she was swatting away flies. "We're just stopping the investigation like that?" She said it like she had been slaving over the case all year.

March shot her a look. Madeleine turned her nose up.

"No," I said, even though my heart slowly deflated as I imagined them detecting without me. "You guys should definitely keep investigating." Barkley and Lobster and Lenny needed help, even if I wasn't going to be the one to give it.

Catelyn Monsen and another one of Madeleine's soccer friends passed our group, eyeing us like we were a herd of mythical creatures. It was their second lap around the playground.

Madeleine didn't seem to notice. "Sounds good to me," she said. "Did anyone find anything in their search last night?"

March and CindeeRae shook their heads.

"I didn't understand half this stuff." Pushing her way onto the edge of the bench, Madeleine practically sat on top of me, and I scooted over to give her room. She splayed the file folder on her lap. Maybe I wouldn't miss out on any more detecting; maybe we had finally reached a dead end.

Madeleine rambled on and on as she thumbed through her papers, talking about what everyone already knew about the case. When her copy of the receipt slipped from the folder and fell to the ground, I remembered what I had noticed the night before. I plucked up the sheet and studied it again. "Where do your parents buy dog food?"

"King Soopers on the other side of Federal,"

CindeeRae answered. "It's, like, two minutes away."

"Mine too," Madeleine agreed.

"I think it's the closest store to our neighborhood," I said. "So why would Crowley go to a King Soopers in the opposite direction? On Forty-Third Avenue?" I pointed to the address on the receipt: *5302 W. 43rd Avenue.*

"Because he was visiting someone—" Madeleine was not following my train of thought.

March interrupted her, "Because it's closer to doggie-holding headquarters."

"Exactly!" I said.

"Great." Madeleine slumped back against the bench next to me. "So we know he got dog food at another King Soopers. How does that help us?"

I leaned forward, looking at each of them as I asked, "What if the address of doggie-holding headquarters is close to where Dickinson Street and Forty-Third Avenue intersect?"

CindeeRae's eyes lit up.

"Does anyone have a phone?" March asked. "Let's look it up."

Madeleine took her phone from her back pocket, finally catching on. She punched at the screen and gaped for a second. "You won't believe this." She waved her phone as if it were a wand. "The intersection of Dickinson Street and Forty-Third Avenue is where Magic Planet is."

Magic Planet was an abandoned amusement park

downtown, about fifteen miles from Lakeview Park. It would take thirty minutes to get there on bike.

"That's it, right?" CindeeRae asked. "Magic Planet must be where they're keeping the missing dogs."

"It's unlikely," March said. "Those two things are probably not even related."

"Maybe," I said. "Maybe not. But there's a chance that they might be, right? Either way, we don't have anything else to go on—"

"Plus," Madeleine interrupted, "Magic Planet would be a great place to hold the dogs. It makes sense."

I had gone to Magic Planet when I was seven—the last year it'd been open—although I couldn't really remember it. Dad talked me into riding the Jack Rabbit, a rickety roller coaster that looked like a white toothpick tower from far away. After passing through a tunnel shaped like a mine shaft, I decided it was easiest not to see where we were going, and I kept my eyes closed the rest of the way. As Madeleine, March, and CindeeRae argued whether or not they should visit Magic Planet that afternoon, I felt like I had reached the same place in the case; I wanted to close my eyes the rest of the way.

Suddenly I realized everyone had stopped talking to look at me. "So," March said. "Are you coming with us?"

I remembered Mom's face when she grabbed my Sleuth Chronicle, contorted with disappointment and anger. "I'm not allowed."

"You're not allowed to go on a bike ride?" Madeleine flipped through the pages in her folder without looking at them. "Because when you told us what happened, it didn't sound like you were grounded from bike rides with friends."

Catelyn and the girl passed again, and this time Madeleine saw them. "Should we meet at March's house after school?" she asked quickly, directing the question to March and CindeeRae. Had I lost my place on the team already, replaced by Lenny's best friend? My stomach twisted as I watched them.

"Yes!" CindeeRae's eyes seemed to hold a Lobster-shaped reflection.

"I don't know, guys." March looked at me, and I knew he didn't want to do any detecting without me.

"See you after school," Madeleine called over her shoulder, not waiting for March to deliberate. She ran to catch up with her friends.

CHAPTER TWENTY-NINE

After school I dropped my backpack in the entry-way and kicked off my shoes. Mom stood at the kitchen counter folding a basket of laundry; she startled when I shut the door behind me.

"What are you doing here?" she asked. "Are you grabbing your bike?"

"I live here?" Not wanting to make Mom any angrier than she had been the night before, I plastered the sweetest of smiles on my face.

"No, I mean . . ." She walked around the counter toward me, and the moment felt very déjà vu, except my Velma costume was in my closet upstairs and not a surprise waiting for me on the bench. "Madeleine Brown called and invited you on a bike ride. I assumed you would grab your bike from the garage and go."

I searched Mom's face for a trace of last night's rage, but she looked perfectly calm. "I thought I was grounded?" I asked.

My mind whirled with more questions than that. Why had Madeleine Brown gone through the trouble of calling Mom so I could join this mission? Did she want me there since I had been the one to get her on the team, or did she finally appreciate my detecting expertise? That last idea made me smile.

"Sweetie." Mom busied herself by sorting through the mail stacked in the cubby by the door, pulling out envelopes and tucking them under one arm. "I don't want you to stop playing with your friends. And I think it's wonderful that you're making new ones." She stopped and looked at me. "What I don't want, however, is you nosing around in police business. I appreciate your curiosity and passion, but it's become dangerous and could get you and March hurt."

I nodded, not trusting myself to say anything. Madeleine's cover was good, obviously convincing, but I was still disobeying Mom by going on this bike ride. The thought pinballed from my brain to my gut, making me feel sick.

"Go on." She motioned toward the garage. "They're waiting for you."

"Thanks, Mom." I hugged her waist and then slipped my shoes back on.

As I rode to March's house, I felt the strange sensation of being both heavy and light. Heavy with the guilt of betraying Mom, and light with the excitement of detecting.

I had never biked farther than ten miles before, except with my parents. Living off Federal, we were usually less than fifteen minutes away from anything interesting by bike. The Denver Exploration Museum for Kids, the Mayan Theater, the Tattered Cover Book Store, and Coors Field, if traffic was good. My parents didn't allow me to cross Federal into the busier areas of downtown without them.

But Magic Planet wasn't downtown. In fact, it was in West Highland, the opposite direction of downtown and about twice as far away as the elementary school. We rode on residential streets with hardly any traffic. Every now and then we passed a skateboarder or a jogger. But when March's bike skidded to a stop at the end of the street, right up against the chain-link fence surrounding

Magic Planet, my stomach erupted in a flurry of butter-flies. I tried imagining that we were just a group of kids exploring an abandoned amusement park. There was no harm in that, right? And it's not like anyone would tell Mom about it.

The metal curve of the Jack Rabbit rose above the fence, but years of overgrown bushes and vines had crowded the chain-link, and it was impossible to see much else.

"This is it?" Madeleine asked.

"The backside of it." March rolled his bike away to the edge of the sidewalk, noticeably agitated to have arrived. "Traffic's busiest at the front, so I thought we'd check the back first."

Madeleine and I laid our bikes on the sidewalk and stepped to the fence. I cupped my hands around my eyes like a telescope and tried to peer through the greenery. Nothing.

We walked our bikes down the sidewalk on West 41st Avenue, checking for breaks in the fence. March and CindeeRae hung back a few paces, the cards on March's spokes suddenly loud in the still afternoon.

March had just started to speak when I noticed a camouflage cover hung from one fence post to another—hard to see because of an overgrown shrub nearly as tall as me lining the fence.

"There." I pointed, my voice a whisper. We all stood and stared at the suspicious panel, as if we expected the camouflage cover to rise like a curtain, and a line of kidnapped dogs to parade out.

"Let's park our bikes," Madeleine said, breaking the spell, and we followed her around the corner of the block, where I began to lock mine against the fence.

"No way," March said, pulling the U-lock from my hand and putting it back in my basket. "We leave them unlocked for a quick getaway."

No one argued.

Madeleine pulled back the camouflage cover to expose a perfect rectangular cut in the fence. She ducked inside, pushing through a canopy of foliage, loudly.

We shushed her from the safety of the other side of the fence. Madeleine waved us in, and the three of us hesitated. It felt like we should hold a debate on the pros and cons of trespassing onto Magic Planet.

"We need a plan," I whisper-yelled at her.

"We're checking things out," she said. "That's our plan."

"That's not good enough," I said as she waved away my concern and disappeared inside.

I turned to March and CindeeRae, anxious to catch up with Madeleine before she did something stupid. "If anything bad happens, we meet back here." That seemed a good addition to the plan. Ignoring the flurry of anxiety in my gut, I pushed back the camouflage and stepped inside the fence.

The cover of trees and the Jack Rabbit towering overhead made it seem much darker than late afternoon. There were no lights in the abandoned amusement park, and the place echoed with the eerie quiet of a haunted alley. CindeeRae and March pushed their way in, the swooshing of brush loud in my ears.

"Now what?" CindeeRae whispered.

"We investigate," Madeleine said, using her outdoor voice. We shushed her again. Even CindeeRae, master of voice projection, knew when to keep it down.

"You're a bunch of chickens." Madeleine walked ahead to a bank of cotton candy and snow-cone booths. From there we could see more of the park, including the Sea Dragon and the Round-Up. Some of the rides had been pulled for reuse at other amusement parks or the new Magic Planet downtown. Darkened gaps marked where the Ferris Wheel, the Wild Cat, and the Sky Ride used to be, as if Godzilla had plucked them from the park and tossed them into the ocean.

We were walking toward the old Magic Summer Theater when a low hum rose in the chill air, followed by a chorus of barking. We stopped, and I turned my ear toward the noise.

"Is that what I think it is?" CindeeRae asked, her green eyes flashing against the park's shadows.

"Let's go." Madeleine took off toward the sound, her black Converses slapping the pavement.

"She's crazy." March grabbed my elbow as I tried to follow after her. "We still need to be careful even if she isn't."

I stopped and looked around. He was right. This wasn't how you launched a successful mission, I thought, watching Madeleine stomp down the park's main thoroughfare and out of view.

CindeeRae, March, and I cut across the overgrown grass surrounding the backside of the shelter for the food court and carnival games. The barking came from inside that building.

Hugging the wall, we slunk around to the side, where we could just barely see the carousel pavilion across the path. White Christmas lights hanging from the eaves suddenly lit up against the late afternoon.

"That sound is a generator," March whispered. "That's how they're powering the lights."

"Who?" CindeeRae asked. "And for what?"

Her question hung in the air.

I tiptoed down the side of the building, March and CindeeRae following, and peeked around the corner to see what was under the shelter.

Dogs, big like Genki, were chained to shelter columns. Straw had been dumped on the cement floor, and each of them had cleared a perfect circle around their posts. The chains were just short enough to prevent them from reaching one another, and each post included a metal dish and a ratty blanket.

Once CindeeRae realized where the dogs were, she stepped into the open to search for Lobster.

Across the path, I could see the whole carousel pavilion, only it no longer housed a carousel, but a makeshift fight-ring on a platform, the railing spotted with blood.

I pulled CindeeRae back. "Those are fight dogs. Lobster won't be here."

We ducked behind the wall again, watching for Madeleine. Crouched low, I peeked around the shelter wall.

Crowley walked inside with another man.

CHAPTER THIRTY

I reeled back and landed on my butt, pressing a hand to my mouth to stop myself from yelping. March looked to see what had frightened me, and when he recognized Crowley, I had to dig my fingers into his arm so he wouldn't take off without us. If we moved too fast, we'd all be caught. I shuddered at the thought.

After my breathing steadied, I eased back to my perch at the wall, trying to listen in, but their conversation was lost to the sound of the generator and maybe even the beating of my heart. Still, all I could think was that we had been right: Crowley had been part of the dognapping ring all along.

I dropped to my knees and crawled closer, trying to hear what they were saying. March grabbed at my ankle, but I kicked him away. They shifted as they talked, their backs mostly to me. Two bar tables stood between us, but if they moved just right they would see me.

"You're being sloppy," Crowley said. "All the news recently has been about dogfights. The police uncover you, and we're not far behind."

The man's voice rose in anger. "Our operation's tight—you worry about yourself and keep the big dogs coming our way. We'll be fine."

"I can't get them to you any faster," Crowley said. "We have a strict process. I'll note the request for more, but you look full here." There was a pause, and my breath caught in my throat as I waited for them to move. They stayed put. "What's your capacity at the warehouse?"

"We need at least ten more," the man grumbled, an angry edge still in his voice.

"Okay. We'll work on it."

I caught a glimpse of Madeleine peering around the carousel pavilion, and my heart seemed to explode in my chest.

"I'll call with news," Crowley said, and ducked out the shelter, away from the carousel. The other man followed him to the path but then turned in the opposite direction, toward the old log-barrel ride. I stood as soon as it looked like the coast was clear.

March and CindeeRae raced toward me, and the

dogs pulled at their chains and barked at us, baring their teeth. We backed away from them, moving deeper into the shelter. Most were pit bulls with clipped tails and ears, their fur spotted with blood. One of the biggest dogs seemed to be missing an eye, or it was just too swollen for me to see. I swayed, dizzy.

The barking echoed under the tin roof and vibrated in my chest. Madeleine, hearing the commotion, waved at us from the pavilion. "I'm over here, guys," she yelled.

My stomach dropped. I grabbed CindeeRae's and March's hands and pulled them to the back of the shelter and out the opposite side, the chains clanging as the dogs strained toward us. Motioning for Madeleine to follow, we rushed down the path, just as two men—the one we'd seen with Crowley, and another man—charged at us from the log-barrel ride. The man who had been with Crowley was short and had thick arms covered in tattoos, while the other was tall and skinny with a scraggly beard that he had braided into a tiny point.

We shot the other way, sprinting toward the exit behind the Jack Rabbit. Madeleine's soccer speed put her in the lead, while March fell behind. As we were passing the old Magic Summer Theater, I looked back over my shoulder for him and realized he had fallen, his leg caught in a hole from an upended fence post.

I veered off, looping around the Viking ship to get back to March, CindeeRae following me. As the men drew closer, their feet pounding on the pavement, Madeleine appeared like a ghost, dragging March to his feet just as the men rounded the corner to the old Magic Summer Theater. With superhero strength, Madeleine wrapped March's arm around her shoulder and ran down the path with him like they were competing in a three-legged race. CindeeRae and I changed direction and caught up to them just as they slipped through the break in the fence.

Madeleine screamed as we ran to our bikes, "Kidnappers! We're being attacked! Help!"

No one followed after us as we pedaled home, our bikes weaving in and out of the bright streetlights.

Madeleine called the police tip line from her cell phone as we huddled around her in March's basement. We listened as she told them about the dogs chained up inside Magic Planet, and the big men lumbering about. She hung up when they asked for her name and number, and we all stood breathless for a few seconds.

Because it was dark, our parents came to pick us up, and I walked with Madeleine to our bikes parked in

March's driveway. Her mom sat in the front of a big SUV, talking on the phone while Madeleine lifted her kickstand with the toe of her shoe.

"You're not bad to hang out with," I said. "So why are you so mean and bossy?"

She stopped walking her bike to look at me, and I thought her expression was probably the same one she gave soccer opponents trying to score a goal. "You try being the biggest kid in your class *and* Korean. When I was younger, kids picked on me all the time." She shrugged. "They don't anymore."

There was no excuse for being mean, but I understood what it was like to be different. "Well, I just wanted you to know that I think you're brave." I busied myself with my kickstand. "And you saved March today, so . . . thank you."

Even in the darkness I could see a grin curl at her lips. "You're kinda bossy, too," she said. "But I think you're a good detective."

It was almost a direct quote of the first item from the friendship list I had written down for Mrs. Hewitt last week. We shared a smile as her mom stepped from the SUV. I watched Madeleine roll her bike to the car and remembered the day I tried pelting her with a Jolly Rancher but hit our music teacher instead. I snorted.

Madeleine turned around and looked at me just as

Dad rounded the corner of Colonial. "What?" she asked.

I repeated a line from our detention song. "'Teacher thinks that I sound funny . . .'"

Madeleine added, "'But she likes the way you sing.'"

"Unlikely," I blurted, and this time Madeleine laughed, too.

"Totally unlikely," she agreed.

I waved to her as I rode my bike toward Dad.

CHAPTER THIRTY-ONE

Dressing like Velma made me walk with a bit more sass, my red Mary Janes snapping on the school tiles as March and I headed up the stairs to our classrooms. After Madeleine had told me I made a good detective, I had decided to wear my Velma Dinkley costume with pride. But even the added confidence hadn't helped me shake the feeling that our Magic Planet discovery only meant we still had no idea where the doggie-holding headquarters were.

March, dressed like Steve Jobs, asked, "The usual T-or-T tonight?"

"I don't know. Mom and Dad are nervous about the dognapper situation. Maybe we can tag along with

Maggie?" We reached the top of the stairs, where kids mingled in clusters, showing off their costumes.

"Two stormtroopers," I said, unable to help myself from playing slug-bug Halloween.

He cocked his head to the side, searching for the second stormtrooper. It took him a while because Sandy McAllister had colored the entire thing pink. "Oh," March said. "A stormtroopress."

"That's not a thing."

"Three cats," he said. "I don't know if Maggie's taking anyone tonight. She said something about being too old for that. Plus, there's a party somewhere."

Maggie had been taking half the Winters kids around for a few years, since Marshall and Candy felt outnumbered with all of them. Since we were ten, March and I had gone trick-or-treating alone because the neighborhood was usually busy enough that our parents didn't worry. We worked from my house on Honeysuckle to Morningside, where we stopped at the Furman house to eat homemade pizza, which they pulled hot from a stone oven on their back patio. Then we hit the Colonial loop before stopping at the Rollinses' on Summer Glen; they were a cute old couple who always dressed like mummies and served hot chocolate until eight thirty. We would finish Summer Glen, drop back to Honeysuckle, and end at my house by nine.

"My parents could shadow us from half a block away."

I imagined them as Goku and Wonder Woman, holding hands and flirting down the block. Ew.

"Okay." The bell rang and March gestured toward the bathroom. "Oh, and if I see a Scooby-Doo, can I call it a twofer since Velmer is on his team?"

I turned around to see Sky Mendelson dressed in a full-body Scooby costume, complete with a doggie hood that covered his head.

I rolled my eyes and turned back to March. "*Vel-ma*," I clarified, drawing each syllable out like a separate word. The more we talked, the edgier I felt. "Plus, it's not 'Scooby's Team.' It's called Mystery Incorporated."

March shrugged, no longer interested in that part of the conversation. "It's my theory that kids wearing animal costumes get more treats at T-or-T."

"Trick-or-treating!" I said. "Gah! You are such a geek."

March's brows drew together, hooding his eyes. "Halloween makes you grouchy."

I turned and walked to my classroom without saying good-bye.

During lunch recess, we spread the newspaper on the pavement outside the foursquare courts, and CindeeRae read aloud the article about the dogfighting bust. A picture of three men, handcuffed and lying on the ground, was displayed above the fold. Four of the ten dogs had already been returned to their owners, while the rest were being treated by a veterinarian. There were no pictures of the dogs. We knew why.

After CindeeRae followed the story to page five and read to the end, she crumpled the paper into a big wad and threw it over her shoulder. I scrambled after it, tearing the article from the paper and folding the sheets neatly so I could put it in the Sleuth Chronicle later.

"We're no closer to finding our own dogs than we were before." CindeeRae sat with her knees pulled under her chin, cat hood covering her face.

"And it just keeps getting more dangerous," March said. "We should tell our parents. We have enough information now—they would believe us."

"But we still don't know where they're keeping the dogs." I stuffed the folded newspaper into the waistband of my Velma skirt.

"Maybe they missed something at Crowley's house," March said. "If we told the police we were the ones that called, and that we saw him there, maybe they'd search again."

March was right; maybe it was time to come clean and let the police know what we had discovered about Crowley, if they would even believe us.

"Officer Rhodes thinks I made everything up, remember?" I said. "I'm not a credible witness."

The roar of the playground behind us seemed to grow as we sat silent.

"This is stupid." Madeleine stood, her pirate scarf falling to cover half her face. She kicked the garbage can next to the school, and a deep echo rang from the bin. I shook my head in frustration. This would be one of the few times I actually agreed with her.

CHAPTER THIRTY-TWO

CindeeRae caught up to us as we reached the flag-pole outside. The ruffling of all the costumes and the hum of Halloween excitement swelled around us, and I wanted to cover my ears against the happy noise. We had no plan, and nowhere to look for new clues.

As I followed them to the bus turnout, I stopped when I recognized a mom standing outside her car in the carpool lane, waving wildly. She was parked three spaces ahead of Madeleine's mom with her dark hair in a perfectly straight bob. Watching her as Madeleine and Catelyn walked past to their own car gave me a chill of déjà vu.

"Hey." CindeeRae pointed. "Isn't that *your* mom?"

My mom hadn't picked me up from school

unexpectedly since Papi died two years ago. Papi was Dad's dad, who died in a car accident.

I turned from the carpool lane and ran toward my bus, putting as much distance between me and Mom's news as I could. But I wasn't used to running in the Mary Janes and tripped in the middle of the walkway, my treat bag flying into the air and scattering all around me.

March and CindeeRae hovered above. "Are you okay?" March asked. When I didn't answer, they both dropped to the ground and began picking up the Tootsie Rolls, glow sticks, and spider rings Mrs. Thomas had given us for Halloween. I felt dizzy and confused, as if I had just been spun wildly and released, with no one to catch hold of me.

Madeleine reached me before Mom did, her voice panicked. "What happened?"

My red Velma skirt was torn, and my knees were bleeding, and I pushed the newspaper pages that had fallen from my waistband against my skin to stop it. When Mom reached me, she knelt and asked, "Kazu, are you okay?"

I looked Mom in the eyes. They were red-rimmed.

"Genki?" I knew Mom had come to school because Genki was missing. I don't know how he did it, but Crowley had stolen my dog; he had taken my absolute best friend in the world.

"I'm so sorry," Mom answered, and I ducked my head to my bloody knees and cried.

CHAPTER THIRTY-THREE

I sat in the front seat of the car, feeling like my chest had been split open with blunt-edge scissors. March and CindeeRae had missed their buses and sat in the backseat, their silence somehow making the car quieter than it would've been without them.

"Sweetie." Mom rested her palm on my leg. "Genki jumped the fence, and I thought he was chasing squirrels again, so I drove to all his favorite places and couldn't find him. When I went to the police station to file a report, they said four other dogs had been taken in the last two days. It seems the dognappers strike in batches."

Mom watched me process the information. I turned my head toward the window.

I had almost forgotten March and CindeeRae were

in the car when CindeeRae spoke, unexpected and loud like a megaphone. "Lobster was taken from my backyard one night. He's purebred, so Daddy thinks the dognappers may have sold him to a puppy mill. But we'll get him back when they catch the dognapper."

I couldn't help but wonder what Crowley would do with Genki. He was a big dog, bred to fight, and if you didn't know about his social anxiety disorder, you might think he snacked on Chihuahuas. What if Crowley sold Genki to dogfighters? Or maybe worse, what if he became a lab dog, injected with all sorts of things that would turn him into a Frankendoggie?

"Madeleine's dog was taken, too," I mumbled to Mom under my breath.

"What, sweetheart?"

March answered for me, like he had last week when I stopped talking. "Madeleine Brown, this girl at our school. Her dog disappeared two nights ago from Sleepy Hollow. She was a wreck." His voice turned on the last word when he realized I was kind of a mess, too, but instead of changing it, he just mispronounced it. *Wrecky.*

By the time Mom pulled in front of CindeeRae's house, CindeeRae had invited herself over for a Halloween party later that night, since she couldn't go trick-or-treating, and I no longer wanted to. Mom promised lots of candy, and maybe a scary movie. I imagined March's tormented push against the back of my seat at the thought of surrendering his last eligible night of T-or-T. But when Mom parked in front of his house, he got out of the car and yelled, without a hitch, "See you at the Halloween Par-tay, Kazu."

It was the most ordinary sentence in the world, but it made my eyes sting as I watched March bob toward his front door.

March, CindeeRae, and I sat in my basement, the old *Poltergeist* movie playing in the background as we sifted through piles of candy on the floor. My parents had dumped one pitcher full into our trick-or-treat bags at the beginning of this impromptu Halloween party, and now we halfheartedly traded unearned candy that looked too prim and glossy in the wrappers.

The basement was dark, with a small end-table light flickering like a heartbeat. Any other Halloween, it would have spooked me, but tonight, all I could think about was Genki.

We sat in a circle. "Are you okay?" CindeeRae asked, the first thing that any of us had said since dumping the candy and sorting through it with indifferent fingers.

The question triggered my tear ducts, so instead of answering I just shook my head. March, sitting

216

cross-legged next to me, bumped my knee with his, and it was just like a hug.

"I like your posters," CindeeRae said, trying to change the subject.

Our walls were covered with Japanese movie posters: *My Neighbor Totoro, Seven Samurai, Battle Royale, Ring (Ringu),* and *Godzilla, King of the Monsters.* My parents had a thing for classic Japanese cinema.

"Thanks," I said. Our basement looked like a make-shift cinema room, with dark red walls and black leather recliners. To make it kid-friendly, my parents had gotten a ginormous Lovesac that was pushed up against the back of the room, but Genki always used it as a kingly dog bed whenever we came downstairs.

We turned back to the television, watching as one of the poltergeist hunters tried to peel his face off in the bathroom after rummaging through his host's refrigerator. We watched for another hour, clear until the clown doll came alive and pulled the boy under the bed.

"Genki's probably still in Crowley's van," I said. We knew Crowley took the dogs, but we also knew he didn't keep them in his house. As the *Poltergeist* boy's kicking legs disappeared beneath the bed and his sister watched horrified, my two friends turned to me.

"Probably," March said. "But he won't be for long."

CindeeRae grabbed my hand and squeezed. Less

217

than three blocks from where we sat, Genki might be huddled, terrified and alone, with no dining room table or blanket nest to soothe him. What would Crowley do with my puppy?

"We should sneak into his garage," I mumbled, barely able to hear the words myself. "And see if he's there."

From the television, the *Poltergeist* mom screamed "No, no, no!" as some invisible force dragged her up the wall and across the ceiling.

March's head snapped up. "What?"

"Maybe we could save him—tonight."

CHAPTER THIRTY-FOUR

"We could get killed," March whispered.

I shook my head. "All he cares about are the dogs. And tomorrow Crowley will probably take Genki somewhere . . ."

CindeeRae fiddled at a pile of Dubble Bubble bubble gum she had made. She flattened her hand in the middle of the pile and shook it. Pieces shot across the carpet and one hit the wall with a thud.

"Sorry." She ducked her head as she searched for the missing piece of gum. "That just sounds really dangerous."

March's face was white and his eyes wide, but he didn't shift his gaze from mine. There were no other arguments to make, and this problem was too big to solve with Janken. The TV blared as *Poltergeist* Mom tried to save her kids.

"Okay," March said.

"What?"

"You're right," he said. "Let's do it."

My heart dropped to my gut; I hadn't expected March to give in that easily. Alone I might not be able to sneak into Crowley's garage and rescue Genki. But now, with him, I couldn't backtrack on my own plan. A plan that came from a flaming thought in my brain—a thought I had spoken without really thinking through.

"Should we invite Madeleine?" I asked.

March and CindeeRae looked at each other. I could tell that after what happened at Magic Planet, March had softened toward Madeleine. She had saved him, after all.

"Yes." He dug his flip phone from his pocket, where he had added her number yesterday.

"So," I said, without enthusiasm. "Tonight we save Genki?"

CindeeRae unwrapped the bubble gum and dropped it into her mouth, chewing loudly. "My mom's totally not going to be okay with this."

I hadn't gotten any sleep after they left, watching the minutes click away on my alarm clock. My bed was too big without Genki, and I twisted myself up in the blankets trying to get comfortable as I thought about our plan. March and I had done a lot of crazy things as detectives, but sneaking into someone's garage was the craziest.

Once we had decided to rescue Genki, we planned out our mission—Operation: Save the Van Dogs—from my basement floor with Madeleine on speakerphone. We would meet at March's gate and cut through all four backyards separating the Winterses' house from the Crowley house, since the streetlights seemed extra glaring when you were doing something suspicious. We were prepared to pick the lock to the back door of his garage and even the back door of his house if we needed to find the van key to unlock his dognapping van. Madeleine had volunteered to sit outside as lookout, ready to call the police from her bedazzled cell phone in case we got caught.

As the seconds ticked away, I thought of all the things that could go wrong before I even reached the front door of *my* house, each of them ending with getting caught by my parents. Imagining the anger that would bloom on Mom's face if she caught me sneaking out to do more investigating was enough to make me dizzy. Luckily, Mom and Dad were both deep sleepers and didn't seem to stir as I crept by their open bedroom, down the stairs, and out the front door.

Turned out, my old black dance unitard and matching hoodie worked well as a snooping outfit.

March had waited for us at his fence, leading everyone through the side gate to his family's backyard, where we now huddled on the porch.

March wore his dark Steve Jobs turtleneck, the white apple on his chest glowing like a target. CindeeRae and Madeleine both wore black, too, except Madeleine's sweatpants had a white stripe down the sides. I had pulled the drawstring on my hoodie so tight it closed around my face, and my hot breath blew back at me. We lingered by the grill, which sat on the wraparound porch cluttered with lawn chairs and doggie toys. March pulled a ski mask over his face, but Madeleine stopped him when he began to put on a navy marshmallow jacket. The fabric rubbed together like packing peanuts.

"It's cold." Even though he whispered, his voice seemed to echo off the cinder-block wall separating his backyard from Lincoln Street.

"The adrenaline will keep you warm," she said. "That coat's like a burglar alarm."

He shrugged it off and hung it around one of the plastic chairs. I handed them each a Zoo Crew pack loaded with all the spy gear: flashlight, pocketknife, binoculars, and kazoo. We also each had plastic bags loaded with a lock-pick set: two bobby pins bent to act as a lever, a lock pick, plus a handful of extra bobby pins in case we needed replacements. I gave them each a headlamp, too.

We slung the packs onto our shoulders and snapped

the lamps over our headgear. I rubbed my mittened hands together even though I wasn't cold. My fear radiated like a heater in my chest, burning my cheeks and arms.

"We move slowly," I said. I had thought about our backyard strategy all night. "We'll creep along the back fence in case anyone is still awake in the houses. Crowley's neighbor is the only one with a dog, but they keep it inside. If it starts to bark, run as fast as you can to his yard." Everything else had been decided in the basement a few hours ago.

"Ready?" I asked, the pulse in my ear thrumming. How did you get your legs to move when you knew they were taking you to danger?

Everyone but March nodded. His wide eyes peered at me from underneath the ski mask, his dark lashes blinking rapidly as if trying to relay a message via Morse code.

"We don't say anything unless we have to, okay?" I shot them each a serious glance.

This time March nodded, too, a little longer than everyone else, and for a second I worried he'd faint before we even made it to Crowley's house.

We climbed over the first fence—a shabby wooden number no higher than my stomach. The moon was a sliver—God's fingernail, Dad always called it—but it was still bright enough to cast a blue glow on the string of backyards separating March's house from Crowley's. The first two plots were tidy little squares with neat borders around the grass and flower beds. The third had no grass at all, the earth upended to create a mini BMX track. And the last yard, Crowley's neighbor with the yipping dog, looked like a graveyard for summer junk. The owner had laid to rest a broken kiddie pool, a handful of tricycles and Big Wheels, a push mower, garden gnomes, and enough folding chairs for an outdoor wedding. The grass, long and stiff, grew tall around it.

We kept along the back wall when we could, but there were stacks of wood against the fence that forced us from our cover, and we stalked in the open where the blue moonlight made the white apple on March's turtleneck glow like a lantern. We had just reached the far back corner when the hem of CindeeRae's black jeans caught the leg of a folding chair leaning in a stack against the shed, and they fell with a crash. She gasped, and a series of fireworks seemed to explode in my chest. Madeleine dove over the fence without us, and March moaned as the dog inside began its snippy call right before a house light flicked on upstairs.

CHAPTER THIRTY-FIVE

The rest of us cleared the fence and rolled onto
the grass of Crowley's backyard to catch up with
Madeleine. Then we crawled to a back door that led to
the garage, our breathing loud and ragged. The neighbor's
porch light snapped on and the sliding glass door opened.
CindeeRae covered her mouth with one hand, and March
turned his wide glowing eyes toward me, shaking his head
like it was all over now. Madeleine glared at us all, and for
a second I didn't know which was more frightening: getting
caught or being the object of Madeleine Brown's wrath.

A man's head peeked out to search the rubble for
criminals, and I sucked in my breath and held it. We flattened ourselves against the backside of Crowley's house;
if the man looked over, he would easily spot us.

The man finally pulled the door closed and turned off the porch light. We waited until the house light also went out before we all let out a big huff of air.

Madeleine slid down the house until her butt rested on the ground. "I'll wait here for you," she whispered, her cell phone clutched in her hands. CindeeRae, March, and I stood frozen against the backside of Crowley's house, looking toward the door. I swayed when I leaned forward. Maybe *I* would be the one to faint. March placed a warm hand on my arm to steady me, and I shook my head to clear the light-headedness. None of Crowley's lights came on. Maybe he was a deep sleeper.

CindeeRae rested her hand on the doorknob. Everything hinged on us being able to easily sneak into the garage and pick the lock into the house if the van wasn't open. I had once watched a news program with my parents that claimed the majority of home break-ins came through the garage where the door to the house wasn't secure. After that program, Mom insisted we change all the locks in the house and add a dead bolt to the door that led from the garage to the kitchen. Hopefully Crowley hadn't watched the same program.

CindeeRae turned the knob, and the door opened with a creak. We stood outside the half-opened door, listening. I heard the hum of a freezer, but nothing more. We tiptoed inside.

I turned on my headlamp and motioned for March and CindeeRae to do the same. A circle of light blinded me for a second, and I squeezed my eyes against it, swatting at March's face so he would turn away.

We stood still for a moment and then looked around, the beams from our headlamps dancing around the garage. Under any other circumstance, March and Mr. Crowley might be besties. The garage was spotless, Crowley's tool bench organized with hooks that included white outlines for every screwdriver, wrench, and hammer. Floor-to-ceiling shelves were stacked with identical boxes, all labeled, and in some cases, dated. Too bad we didn't need camping gear or vinyl records or Mary's hospital bills from 2010 to 2014, because those would all be easy to find.

As I walked to the house door, I nearly bumped into the van parked in Crowley's garage. The image of a dirty van squealing to a stop in front of me flashed in my mind, and I realized this van was the same size and shape the other one had been. I grabbed March's arm and shined my headlamp on the mud-packed side of the dognapping van. Seeing our excitement, CindeeRae came over and stood with us, our shoulders touching. We gaped at the van like we had discovered fossilized dinosaur poop.

"Genki?" My voice filled the garage like an overloud radio accidentally switched on.

A chorus of barks erupted from inside the van. March and I looked at each other, immediately blinded by our headlamps. I pulled mine down to my neck and pushed my hood from my head.

"We've got to go." March breathed the words, quieter than a whisper, and began pulling on my arm. We had been prepared to pick the lock to Crowley's house if we needed the keys to open the dognapping van. Now I felt stupid. Why hadn't we expected the dogs to make any noise before we could even get them out?

"I'm not leaving until we get Genki," I said, yanking on the passenger door handle. The van was locked, but I activated the alarm, which echoed in the garage.

March covered his ears with his hands, and I ran around the van, testing each door. CindeeRae cupped her hands around the driver's window, then jumped back, startled. I took her place, pressing my nose against the window.

It was Genki.

He lunged at the window, pedaling his paws against the glass, and I pressed my hands harder against the surface, wishing I could get to him. The scruff of his neck was dark and matted. Had Crowley already dug the microchip from the back of his neck?

The back door opened and the light snapped on. I dropped to the floor, looking around for March and CindeeRae, who had ducked, too.

On the ground, half-hidden beneath the van, lay a manila folder with the label *Processes and Procedures* written in slanty script. I grabbed it and shoved the folder under my hoodie. March raised his eyebrows, hands still plugging his ears, and I shook my head, uncertain why I thought the folder so important.

"What the . . ." Crowley yelled over the alarm, scanning the garage before he caught sight of us.

James Crowley stood at the hood of the van, less than five feet from where we crouched. He wore flannel PJ bottoms and a white tank top, showing off his massive shoulders.

The three of us stood, close enough that our arms rubbed together. I looked past Crowley to the back door of the garage, Madeleine standing in the door frame with her phone clasped in one hand like a bomb detonator. If we tried to run, he would easily block our way and probably lock us in his basement while the car alarm covered our screams. As if reading my thoughts, Crowley pointed a key at the van and silenced the noise. The garage echoed with Genki's angry barking.

"My papergirl," he said, like he had just discovered the punchline to a funny joke, "delivers to my back door now?"

He stepped toward us, and we scrambled backward, barely staying on our feet as we reached the back of the van. CindeeRae took the lead, inching us to the other side of the garage while March pulled his flip phone from his back pocket and tried accessing the call screen, not trusting Madeleine to the job.

"Listen very carefully." Crowley's voice echoed in the garage as the three of us wound around the van. Genki leaped at each window we passed, his bark growing hoarse. "We're going to pretend like this, right here, is a little nightmare. It'll stop once you climb back into your beds tonight. I'm not sure I can promise as much for your dog."

We reached the hood of the van, with enough room that one quick dash would take us away from Crowley. And Genki.

Crowley's voice rose. "Leave now and your puppy will be sent to a happy place." He placed the palm of his hand on the driver's window. Genki snapped at it, his teeth glinting in the low light of the garage.

Crowley continued. "But tell anyone what you've seen tonight . . ." He pulled his hand away from the driver's window and pretended to lunge at us. We jumped. March dropped his phone and it skidded under the van. "And you'll never see your dog again."

Genki moved to the passenger seat, and even through the tinted windows, I could see his paws slipping on the dashboard as his eyes locked on mine. My chest felt like it was collapsing. If I couldn't save Genki, I had to be sure he wouldn't go somewhere bad, somewhere scary. My legs heavy, I backed toward the door, my cheeks slick with tears. March and CindeeRae backed away with me.

"I'm so sorry, Genki," I cried, fumbling through the garage door. I only started to run when March grabbed my hand and pulled me toward the fence. CindeeRae and Madeleine ran ahead, stopping only to wave us on. As we picked our way back to March's house through the cold, dark air, I could hear Genki's bark fade into the night behind us.

CHAPTER THIRTY-SIX

Mom shook me awake, the overhead light glaring. My back faced her, but I could tell I had slept in. The morning was already churning with light and movement. Who had done my paper route?

"Kazu." She placed a cool palm on my forehead. "Are you sick?" I rolled over to face her and shook my head, realizing as I did that it throbbed. Her eyes widened at the sight of me.

"What?" My voice croaked as I spoke, like my throat was giving out.

"Your eyes," she said. "They're swollen."

My early morning mission with the gang came rushing back at me, and I remembered that Crowley still had Genki. The memory of him threatening to hurt my dog, while Genki bravely stood guard in the front of the dognapping van, made my stomach turn. Tears pooled in my eyes, and I pushed my fists against my face to hide it. My eyelids were puffy and tender, and I realized I must have been crying in my sleep.

"It's been a hard week, and you're sick," she said. "No school today."

At first I wanted to resist, but there was no reason to go to school. March, CindeeRae, and Madeleine would be upset about the mission, and without any more clues, we would be unable to plan another one.

I nodded at Mom. Right now I just wanted to bury myself under the covers and forget what had happened. I was done with detective work. Every mission we planned failed, and now Genki's safety might depend on me quitting forever.

Mom bent toward me and kissed my forehead. The gesture made me want to crawl into her lap and cry.

"Would you like some mugicha with your breakfast?" she asked. "It'll chase away the fever."

I nodded. Mugicha was a roasted barley tea popular in Japan. In the winter Mom served it warm, and she prepared some every time I was sick.

"Well," she said. "You get some rest, and I'll put a pot of mugicha on."

After taking my temperature—99.9—Mom went to the kitchen to make tea, and I got up to grab a lighter blanket from the floor. A manila folder dropped from my hoodie, and I bent to pick up the single sheet of paper that had slipped out.

It was a list, numbered one to eleven. Scratchy sentences written in what looked like another language matched the handwriting on the folder's label: *Processes and Procedures*. In my frightened flight home hours earlier, I had forgotten about the folder, which was bent in the middle from me sleeping on it.

Shoving the folder under the bed, I wrapped myself in the thin flannel throw and curled into a ball, the familiar smell of Genki stinging my eyes.

Mom knocked on my door before opening it enough to poke her head inside my room. "Are you awake?" she asked.

I nodded.

"Your friends are here to check on you." Usually Mom was strict about sick days, not allowing anyone to visit in case I was either faking or contagious. It seemed all rules were disregarded once a lousy dognapper swiped your puppy.

"They're here now?" I didn't have anything to say to them. The mission had failed, and our dogs were still gone.

"All three of them."

I almost wished Mom's sick rule still applied. "Okay," I said, my voice low and hoarse.

They marched in with their arms to their sides and shoulders slumped. Mom eyed us cautiously as she backed out of my room, shutting the door softly behind her.

"Hey, Kazu," March said. "I brought your homework." He set a folder on the edge of my bed.

"Thanks?" Did he not know me? The last thing I wanted on a sick day was my homework.

CindeeRae's hands were clasped in front of her. "I'm sorry it didn't go well last night."

"Okay, okay," Madeleine interrupted, taking a step forward in her black-and-red soccer socks. "We feel bad that you're sick, or whatever. But we still need to figure out where the dogs are."

The envelope rested beneath my bed, with information that was probably related to the case. It would be a lie to say we didn't have any more clues, nowhere to look for the holding location. But risking another mission could put Genki in danger, and so far none of our missions had been successful. It seemed the only thing we were good at was getting into more trouble.

I shrugged. "What can we do? We don't know where they're keeping the dogs, and the police already don't believe us about Crowley, so what's the use?"

Madeleine's lips tightened into a thin line and her eyes narrowed. "We can't give up."

"Look." CindeeRae stepped forward in an attempt to referee the situation. "We just thought you should know that my aunt said they're zeroing in on some guy. She couldn't really give me details, but she said he'd been reported for suspicious behavior already. Maybe they're onto Crowley?"

Before last night, that information would have been exciting. But now that Crowley had threatened Genki, I couldn't put his life in any more danger by helping the police or participating in another klutzy mission.

"We should just let the police do their jobs." I couldn't meet any of their eyes. "It's what they do, right? Find the bad guys."

"But what if our dogs are long gone by then?" CindeeRae's stage voice was back, but this time she definitely wasn't acting.

I pulled the covers closer to my neck. "I should probably get some sleep. I'll see you guys tomorrow?"

CindeeRae and Madeleine held fisted hands at their sides. What did they expect from me? I had done everything we could so far to save the dogs. It wasn't my fault it hadn't worked. There was nothing left to do.

My cheeks flushed as I remembered the envelope under my bed. Well, *they* didn't have to know about that.

The girls stomped from my room, and March stayed back in the clutter, looking down at my floor. "I understand, Kazu," he said without looking up. "It'll be okay. You'll all get your dogs back."

Once March left, I pulled the envelope from its hiding spot and rolled onto my side, curling around our only clue like it was a floatie and my bed the rocky ocean.

Last summer, when we were ten, March and I sent secret messages to each other using a Caesar Shift, which is a code where you line two streams of the alphabet together. To help me decode his messages and code my own, March made a cipher wheel with two paper plates, one smaller than the other, and fastened together in the center with a paper fastener. Each circle had a line of the alphabet around the rim and by lining them up, we could create our own cipher.

Ours had been cipher 5, which meant the inner alphabet moved five places to the left: *A* became *V, B* became *W,* and *C* became *X.* When I delivered papers in the morning, I would drop off my message and pick up March's. And because only juicy messages were sent with a Caesar Shift, I learned that March's dad had gambled away part of their tax refund playing internet poker, Maggie had a boyfriend and March had caught them kissing on the lips, and Max and Miles had flushed all their fish down the toilet in an experiment to see if they would end up in the irrigation ditch that ran through their backyard.

Using the cipher wheel March had made, I halfheartedly studied the code used in the clue I had found in Crowley's garage, mostly because it was more interesting than the homework March had brought over. I had tried ciphers one through thirteen before my pencil lead wore down to a nub.

The endless combinations probably extended way beyond the Caesar Shift. Crowley could have used a kazillion ciphers, shifts, and codes, and by the time we figured it all out I would be eating DineWise while paying someone to rake *my* leaves and push *my* garbage to the curb. It didn't matter; nothing we did ever changed anything. I threw the pencil across the room, and it landed perfectly in the slot from last year's valentines box sitting atop my dresser.

CHAPTER THIRTY-SEVEN

Mom called me down to the dining room before lights-out. A big display sat on the table—a giant diorama for the museum exhibit she had finally started piecing together.

She stood at the head of the table like she was ready to give a presentation to the museum board. Sometimes she practiced like this in front of Dad, and I felt very grown-up to have been invited. Mom motioned for me to take a seat, and I slid into the chair closest to her. I studied the exhibition fragments like disconnected puzzle pieces; it took a few seconds for all the parts to snap into place and make sense.

A banner lining the top of the table read THE EXHIBITION OF ESPIONAGE AND SLEUTHING. My notebook sat in the bottom corner, open to a list of clues on the dognapping ring that I had collected from all my newspaper articles. A tri-fold poster listed spy artifacts with pictures next to each item, including a lipstick pistol, button-hole camera, an Enigma machine for deciphering code, and a hollow silver dollar for carrying secret messages. There was a chain of Post-it notes detailing a case kids could solve, with a long list of clues and where they could be found in the Case Room.

"I hope you don't mind," Mom said, pointing at my Sleuth Chronicle. "But I thumbed through your notebook to see what you were up to and found myself a little inspired. I realized that a detective exhibit would probably be very exciting for kids."

My heart fluttered at the thought of visiting Mom's exhibition, which would definitely be my favorite of all time.

"I thought about what you said." She leaned over and grabbed my notebook, flipping to a spot somewhere in the middle. "About how nothing you like is important unless I like it, too. I think you might have been right about that." She set the notebook down in front of me.

I looked down: あたりまえ was written in bold at the top of the page. *Atarimae*. The Japanese word that described obvious and reasonable behavior, although it also meant the kind of things people do naturally, like a reflex. I had always thought detecting was my atarimae—collecting clues and solving mysteries was like a reflex to me, like Mom's reflex was designing fun and interactive exhibits for kids at the museum.

Mom sat down in the chair next to me. "As I tried to understand why you like studying cases, collecting clues, and solving these crime puzzles, I realized that it was kind of exciting. And I started to wonder what it might be like if we combined the things we both felt were important. That's when I came up with this idea for the next long-term exhibit at the exploration museum." She leaned back and smiled. "I think it's perfect."

Mom had taken all this time to understand something important to me. Even though my heart ached at the Genki-size hole in my life, I couldn't help but smile. "I think it's perfect, too."

"Would you mind being my assistant?" she asked. "We could brainstorm even more ideas—I need your investigative expertise."

I nodded, an airy feeling rising in my chest before I remembered Genki and the achy weight returned. Mom leaned over and pulled me into a hug. "We're going to find Genki," she whispered in my ear, and for a second it felt like she had squeezed all the worry right out of me. And then I imagined Genki stuck in Crowley's dognapping van, and it flooded back.

I studied Mom's display, all the information on gathering clues and solving crime. Could I really give up on finding my puppy when we still had one last clue to follow? If solving crime and saving people was a reflex to me, then that reflex should be supersized when it involved Genki. The least we could do was decipher the code and call the tip line with any information we uncovered.

I imagined my puppy curled in a ball by my feet, anxious for bedtime. He would come home soon; I would make sure of it.

"Let's do this," I said.

I reached March's house fifteen minutes before the bus arrived. His mom seemed surprised to see me so early in the morning. Her short blond hair stuck out from her head in chunky spikes, and it distracted me for a second before I remembered why I was there.

"I need to study with March," I said.

She pointed at the stairs, and I took them two at a time, not bothering to turn around when she asked if I had eaten yet.

"I'm good, thanks."

I barged into March's room, and he jumped from the corner of his bed, where he sat loading his backpack.

"You scared me to death, Kazu." He closed his eyes and let out a soothing sigh while I dropped my bag in the doorway and dashed to the bed. March didn't appear to have slept much. His face was cement gray.

"Remember how I took this from Crowley's garage?"

March's eyes snapped open, and he leaned back like I was passing him a grenade.

"It's coded." I laid the sheet on his lap and pulled the cipher wheel from my notebook. "You've got to figure out what it means before Crowley does something bad to Genki."

"You were right before," March said, his arms folded over his chest. "If we keep getting in his way, Crowley's going to kill *us*."

"You don't have to help, March," I said. "I understand. But what if it were Hopper?"

He sat still, studying the document without touching it. Then, as if surrendering to a chocolate-strong urge, he grabbed the cipher wheel from my hand and began turning it slowly. "Get me a pencil." He had that faraway look in his eye like he had stepped through a geeky portal into a new dimension, with nothing but binary code and Marvel comics.

I grabbed a pencil from the cup on his desk and handed it to him. He scribbled letters above the code, erasing them quickly as he continued to turn the cipher wheel. After a few seconds, he chewed on the eraser and said, "There are hundreds of different codes Crowley could have used. It would take forever to crack this manually."

"What other choice do we have?"

"Maggie."

"What about her?"

"She has code-breaking software. The problem is, she won't do it unless we tell her what it's for."

"What are we waiting for?"

"She'll tell my parents if she thinks we're doing something dangerous."

At this point, we had broken all of our rules, including the last one about avoiding anything that could get us killed. Lying to Maggie about our operation would be easy-peasy.

"I'll handle Maggie," I said, offering a hand to help him stand.

March led me to the bathroom, where Maggie leaned over the sink, spraying something foggy into her hair.

"Hey, Maggie," I said casually, leaning into the door frame and watching her through the mirror.

"What do you want, Kazu?" She set the bottle down and stared at me with her glacier eyes. "You're creeping me out."

"March and I were hoping you'd help us decode this stupid note Sky Mendelson and his friend were passing about March in reading."

"What?" March chirped behind me.

"It's okay, March," I said. "Maggie gets how lame bullies can be."

March pinched my back, squeezing so hard I yelped. "What's up with you two?"

"Nothing," we both said.

"It's just . . ." I folded the sheet in half. "I picked the note out of the garbage, and March is stumped, so I thought you could help."

She snatched the paper from my hand and looked it over. "*Processes and Procedures?*"

"Weird, right?" I toyed with the slack of my backpack strap as I held her gaze.

Her eyebrows dropped, creating a dark line of suspicion above her eyes. Then finally, like March had, she surrendered to the challenge of a puzzle unsolved. "Okay." She shoved the paper into her back pocket and walked from the bathroom, the smell of hair spray chasing her into the hallway. "I will happily trade you one decoded note for ten Reese's Peanut Butter Cups from your Halloween stash."

"What?" March chirped again.

"Deal!" I said, grabbing his arm and pulling him down the stairs and out the door.

The bus rounded the corner toward his stop, and we both slowed down as we crossed the street, watching it pass in front of Crowley's house. Two police cars were parked out front. As the bus looped around the neighborhood and passed Crowley's on the way to school, we saw the cops leave, without Crowley. And without Genki.

My mission plan was more crucial now than ever.

CHAPTER THIRTY-EIGHT

Madeleine leaned back in the cafeteria chair, her face set in a glare. "Why didn't you tell us about this last night?"

I thought they would be happy to hear about the coded sheet and the possibility of more clues, but Madeleine looked ready to battle me in a death match, and I did not have the upper-body strength for that. March fidgeted next to me.

"You can't keep things from us." CindeeRae mirrored Madeleine's body language, arms folded stiffly across her chest. "We're a team, and we all plan missions together."

"Okay." I set my Sleuth Chronicle on the table. Mom had given it back to me the night before. "Then what do you think about my idea?" I had told March about it that morning and he hadn't said anything, which usually meant he would go along with it. The vote might be split, if it came to that, but he would be on my side.

Madeleine shifted in her seat, her posture softening a bit. "I don't understand why you want to go to the police. Aren't we trying to avoid them now, since they don't believe you anymore?"

This part of the plan was a hard sell; I wasn't even sure if it would work. I placed my palms on the table and leaned over in a power pose. "The cops are onto Crowley—they were at his place this morning. The whole operation might shut down if he's arrested, at least until Crowley's team feel safe again. We don't know who else is involved—or even how many there are. And because they're so secretive, it might take the police forever to find all the dogs, if they even do. We have to keep the cops away from Crowley until we find out where they're holding the dogs and where the dogs are sent once they leave headquarters."

"No way," March blurted out. His voice was sharp and not squeaky at all. "Kazu, this is crazy! We've gone through garbage, trespassed in an old amusement park— where I almost got killed, by the way—and snuck into a crazy man's garage. That's enough. I'm done."

I turned to March, surprised at the tone in his voice. CindeeRae and Madeleine stared, too.

"I'm going to the police station alone," I said. "You won't even have to be there."

"I don't care." He threw his hands to his side in what looked like an exaggerated shrug but meant the exact opposite. "You're in charge, and you always demand another mission, deadlier than the ones before. But this time we will probably die. Or maybe you will or CindeeRae will or Madeleine will or I will. But someone's going to die. And I would like to not die, and go to MIT someday!"

He could only say that because *his* dog was safe. No, he would *still* wimp out even if Hopper were missing, too, because he was a chicken head, and I always had to beg him to help.

"You're such a guppy," I said between clenched teeth.

March's face flushed; I have never called him a name before in front of other people. That was like best-friend code or something, and I had just broken it.

"Sheesh." Madeleine stood and adjusted the waistband of her athletic shorts. "Melodrama much, people?"

"Madeleine." CindeeRae touched her sleeve as a warning.

"You're a jerk," March said to me. "I don't know why I ever helped you, anyway."

He turned and stalked out of the cafeteria, my chest tightening with the sound of each foot-stomp. March was serious, and it looked like, for the first time ever, I would have to detect without him.

"So," Madeleine said once he was gone. "Let's plan this mission."

Riding to the police station, I worried my after-school snack might return in liquid form on the backseat of the car. When I told Mom I needed to talk with a detective about the dognapping case, she had convinced Dad to take off work early and come with us. He tapped the steering wheel as he drove, and Mom hummed along to a song on the radio. They were trying too hard to act normal, and instead of looking like a family in a car, we looked like people auditioning for a commercial about a family in a car.

I practiced the confession Madeleine and CindeeRae helped me fine-tune at lunch, gesturing with my hands as I silently moved my lips with the script. I had to distract the police from Crowley. If they showed up at his house again, Genki would be a goner, and we'd never find Crowley's partners or their headquarters. My keen spy skills would be tested with this mission.

Dad parked in front of the police station, and I dragged my feet as I followed them inside, wishing somehow that I could do this alone, without my parents.

Instead of sitting in a dark interrogation room across from "bad cop" Officer Rhodes, like I had imagined, I found myself standing at the police-station counter with Mom and Dad, talking with Detective Hawthorne, who was in charge of the dognapper case.

Detective Hawthorne was tall and wide, even bigger than Dad. When the police officer at the front desk paged him, the detective appeared out of nowhere and walked toward us like a steamroller. I didn't think he would stop in time, and I imagined him barreling into the counter and breaking it like a cardboard tower. He ambled up to some cubbies along the wall, grabbed a file, and then swung back to where we stood, all in a swift series of movements that seemed choreographed. He dropped the file on the counter and shook my parents' hands.

"Kazuko." He pronounced my name perfectly after Dad introduced me. Only those who had known me for a few years could actually say my name right. "How can I help you?" He smiled big enough for me to see his molars. His dark hair curled out at his collar, and the heavy stubble on his face was only visible close up.

"A few weeks ago we talked to a police officer about the dognappings." I coughed into my fist to clear my throat. "Some of the things I told Officer Rhodes weren't exactly true."

"What?" Mom snapped.

"It's okay," Detective Hawthorne said, shooting Mom a glance. "Why don't you tell me about it?"

"The collar we gave you? The one belonging to Barkley? I took it off him the day he disappeared."

Detective Hawthorne opened the file and flipped through a few pages before responding. "Before Barkley disappeared, you were the last one to see him, right?"

"I used to walk Barkley on Mondays, Wednesdays, and Fridays. It was one of my jobs."

"I see." He kept his thumb on a sheet of paper in the file, holding his place. "You must be a very responsible young lady to have a dog-walking business *and* a paper route."

"I'm saving for an iPad." My arms started to itch, and I scratched them over my coat. Detective Hawthorne arched his eyebrows, waiting for me to continue, so I went on.

"I let Barkley off his leash," I said, tears pooling in my eyes because I knew I would have to tell them something even worse than the truth next. "I undid his collar and let him run down the shady path behind Pioneer Village without his leash every time I walked him. But this was the first time he had ever run away from me. I got so scared I threw the leash into the zoo garbage but kept the collar, hoping I'd still find Barkley. But I never did."

"And?" Detective Hawthorne prodded.

"Mr. Crowley's house has always been super creepy, so I thought he probably took all the dogs." I couldn't stop the tears dribbling from the corners of my eyes.

They came down fast and dropped from my chin. "March didn't know. I slipped the collar into Mr. Crowley's garbage can before we searched it. And then I convinced him we should tell our parents Crowley was the dognapper."

"And the receipt?"

"What?" I had forgotten about the receipt. Officer Rhodes had left it behind, so I figured no one else knew about it. Stupid police report.

"The dog food receipt. Remember?"

Mom and Dad both looked at me, their eyes all squinty. It felt as if a trap had closed on my ankle. If I confirmed it came from Crowley's recycled newspaper bags, would he still look suspicious?

"I don't know where it came from," I finally said. "Sometimes I get recycled bags from two or three houses. Crowley was one of the houses that day, but I'm pretty sure I collected bags from other people, too."

Detective Hawthorne's expression was unexpectedly kind. He reached under the counter and grabbed a tissue box. I took a tissue and blew my nose, deciding it best to stay at the police station as long as possible, giving Mom time to calm down.

"You're a detective, right?" he asked.

I nodded, because, duh. Although this single confession probably marked the end of my career. I was an eleven-year-old washout. No one would ever believe I was an honest detective now.

I avoided looking at Mom, afraid her laser gaze might light me on fire. Instead I kept my eyes on Detective Hawthorne.

"There are a few detectives out there who want to solve cases so badly, they'll do whatever it takes," he said. "But planting evidence is a serious offense."

I held the tissue to my eyes because, for the first time in my life, I was getting a lecture I didn't deserve. The skin on my cheeks prickled, and it felt like goose bumps blossomed on my scalp.

"Never compromise your good reputation for a rigged outcome. It's not worth it," he said.

I peeked from behind the tissue and realized the lecture had somehow softened my mother's angry edges.

"You're a brave girl," Detective Hawthorne said softly. "That must have been difficult to share."

He thanked Mom and Dad for stopping by and walked us to the car, chatting about football and the weather, like what had happened was no big deal. He opened the back door for me and watched me climb inside, leaning down to say good-bye.

"You'll make a good detective someday, Kazuko." He lowered his voice. "And just so you know, I haven't ruled out James Crowley as a suspect yet."

He winked before shutting the door, and my stomach lurched.

CHAPTER THIRTY-NINE

That night March stood on my front porch, holding out a manila envelope. "You owe me five Reese's Peanut Butter Cups."

I tentatively took the envelope and held it to my chest. "Did Maggie say anything about it?"

"Just that it was a double transposition cipher like the ones used by both sides of the military in World War Two." March tried to act bored by that information, but it was a stretch. "And also that she's pretty sure *Processes and Procedures* wasn't created by Sky Mendelson and friends."

"Is she gonna rat us out?"

"No," he said. "We gave her chocolate. The deal's solid."

I stepped onto the porch with him and closed the

door behind me, dropping my voice to a whisper even though my parents were watching TV downstairs. "I'm sorry I called you a guppy. But you can't quit the case."

"You're always bossing me around," he said. "And I've helped you with every mission, so I should be like a partner or something, not an assistant."

I could be bossy, I thought, remembering how Madeleine had called me Bossy Jones at her second-grade princess unicorn birthday party. Usually I was bossy because I thought I knew the best way to gather clues or solve a case. But being confident didn't mean I could walk all over my best friend. Or any of my friends.

"You're right." I rubbed my arms as the sun began to go down. "I guess we could be partners in charge?"

"I still think it's dangerous."

"You always think it's dangerous."

"True," he said. "But usually the puzzle we're trying to solve is bigger than the fear of solving it. Until now. Now the fear is bigger."

"So you still won't work the case?"

He rocked back on his heels and studied our porch light, a mass of cobwebs and gnats caught around it. "Maybe we could look at the decoded document first and see if it has any good clues." His eyes cut to the envelope clasped to my chest like a shield.

I opened the door to my house and he followed me upstairs.

I slammed my bedroom door behind us and ripped open the envelope, pulling two folded sheets from inside. Behind the original coded list was a printout with the translation. March stood next to me, his mouth moving silently as he read.

I crumpled up the sheets and tossed them to the floor. "It's about DineWise, not dognapping." Without more clues we'd never find Genki.

"What are you doing?" March picked up the sheets and smoothed them out on my bed, dropping to his knees to study them. "The fact that this doesn't make any sense means it's important. Why would you create some weird, nonsense list and then encrypt it so that people like us wouldn't know what it meant?" He shook the paper at me. "This is just another code we have to break." He had that antsy look, like his body itched all over, and he couldn't keep still.

March read from the printout:

PROCESSES AND PROCEDURES
1. Receive DineWise shipment requests from Withe.
2. Determine course of retrieval, being sure

to avoid high-traffic thoroughfares while following standard DineWise delivery routes.

3. Delay assigned DineWise driver from retrieval route to avoid redundancy.
4. Retrieve shipment.
5. Hold shipment at Lewcroy Storage for 24 hours.
6. Transfer shipment to Withe Brokerage Facility, using standard DineWise transport.
7. Scrub storage facility per standard cleaning protocol.
8. Hold shipment at Withe Brokerage Facility for 72 hours to prepare and repackage.
9. Transfer shipment to buyer using downgraded DineWise vehicle.
10. Scrub Withe Brokerage Facility per standard cleaning protocol.
11. Scrub downgraded DineWise vehicle using standard cleaning protocol.

I sighed. "But Crowley doesn't own a DineWise business, right?"

"Not that I could tell from his bank statements." March paced the room.

But we did find a dirty van parked in his garage, a van about the same size as the DineWise vehicles driving through our neighborhood all the time.

March was already following my train of thought. "What if the dognapping van *is* a DineWise vehicle?" he asked. That was why we were such good partners.

I took the paper from March and followed each line with my pointer finger. "This must be the list of processes and procedures Crowley and his partner use for swiping the dogs."

If the shipment were dogs, then Withe told Crowley which types they needed. Crowley followed a DineWise route, after delaying the real driver, and then used his own DineWise van to swipe the dog—that's why it had been in his garage. That meant Lewcroy Storage was Crowley's house, since we already knew he never kept a dog there for long. And he dirtied the van in order to distribute dogs to buyers, like the angry dogfighters at Magic Planet. Although, as far as I could tell, Crowley had gone a little rogue, swiping dogs like Barkley and Muffin when the van was still dirty from distribution. He was getting a little sloppy.

March was way ahead of me. "If LEWCROY is CROWLEY," he said, his voice squeaky with excitement, "then his partner's name is jumbled up, too—WITHE. And where WITHE is, we'll find doggie-holding headquarters."

My heart seemed to stop beating for a second, and then, when it started again, the pounding was deafening, like Crowley slamming his hand on the driver's window.

To find Genki, we would have to find the Withe Brokerage Facility.

"But who's Withe?" March asked like he was reading my mind.

"What if it's someone we don't even know?" I said. "Then what?"

March paced the room. "I'll search Crowley's desktop again and see what I can find. There may be an e-mail that gives his accomplice away. Withe had to communicate 'shipment requests' somehow, right?"

"What should *I* do?" My pulse thrummed with the thought *new clues, new clues, new clues.*

"Gather all the intel in the Sleuth Chronicle and bring it to school tomorrow." March slid the translation back into the tattered envelope, which he then held under his arm. "We need a new plan if we're going to rescue Genki before he's 'transferred.'"

I could tell March had already done the math in his head. I counted it out, using my fingers when it got tricky. If Withe held the dogs for seventy-two hours, that meant we had three days after breaking into Crowley's garage to save Genki from the partner. Today was the end of day two.

We only had one more day.

I squinted at the paper poking from the pages of a Harry Potter book I had grabbed from Ms. Packer's classroom library. The thicker the book, the easier to hide something inside, I had decided.

Ms. Packer had kicked her heels off under the chair and crossed her nyloned feet atop her desk as she leaned back to read a book of her own. She wouldn't suspect any student in her class of avoiding silent reading time when she was such a sucker for it herself. In fact, today she'd probably have us read for another thirty-five minutes until the bell rang.

I studied the paper. WITHE. We knew who Crowley was, making unscrambling Lewcroy easy. But did we know who Withe was unscrambled? Even with all March's computer hacking, we still hadn't figured it out. Would we ever be able to?

I tapped my pencil on the paper. WITHE. I turned the sheet over and tried unscrambling the code by creating words with each letter. ITHEW, IWETH, THIEW, THIWE, HEITW, HEWIT.

I stopped, my mouth dropping open.

Our music teacher, Mrs. Hewitt, had been at Sleepy Hollow with her wiener dog, Pickles, the night before Halloween, and no kids. Mom had thought that was *interesting* when I knew she really meant *weird*. What if she was only there to scope out the doggie parade and then inform Crowley which ones she needed for the next shipment? Mrs. Hewitt would make the perfect accomplice in Crowley's dognapping ring.

But Hewitt was spelled with two *T*'s, not one. Had they intentionally misspelled her code name to throw the police off even more? Or maybe this code ignored duplicate letters? Either way, I had cracked it and couldn't wait to tell the gang.

"Awesome," I whispered, pumping my fist silently.

"Shhhh!" Sammy Clover, the girl sitting behind me, leaned forward. "Some of us are trying to read, Kazuko!" Her entire face was pinched, and her shiny black hair swept toward me in two sharp points.

"Sorry," I whispered, snapping the book shut before Ms. Packer came over and took my paper away.

"Be nice, Sammy." Lana Mesker leaned into the conversation from her desk to the left of mine. "Her dog got swiped this week."

"How did *you* know that?" I asked, not whispering anymore.

Lana shrugged. "Everyone's talking about it."

Never break Rule #2. "Blabbermouths," I said under my breath.

They looked at each other like I had sworn. Ms. Packer stood at my side. Where had that woman come from? She moved like a cat!

"What's going on, ladies?"

"Nothing," I said a little too loudly, trying to distract

her as I slid the *Processes and Procedures* sheet from the book and back to the Sleuth Chronicle before handing her *Harry Potter and the Chamber of Secrets.* "Just saying that this is a very good book." Sammy and Lana were reading again, or doing a good job pretending. "I highly recommend it."

CHAPTER FORTY

In the cafeteria, I pulled March, CindeeRae, and Madeleine aside and whispered, "I think Mrs. Hewitt is WITHE." Before school had started that morning, March and I briefed CindeeRae and Madeleine on the decoded *Processes and Procedures* document.

CindeeRae's eyes narrowed, and her lips tightened into a thin slit. "Where does she live?"

"Whoa." March held his hand out and then looked at the ceiling, puzzled, stroking his chin like it was covered with a beard.

"She *was* at Sleepy Hollow the night Lenny disappeared," Madeleine said. "She walked behind us in the puppy parade."

"*And* she's creepy," CindeeRae said. "Right? She's so

creepy with the singing and the 'push your air from your diaphragm.'" She tried mimicking Mrs. Hewitt's voice but ended up sounding more like she was talking in slow motion.

"If Mrs. Hewitt is WITHE, we need to act fast," I said.

"Slow down," March said. "We can't jump to conclusions like this." He met my eyes and leaned over the table. "We don't have time to pick the wrong suspect, Kazu. If we chase Mrs. Hewitt and she's doesn't have Genki, our time's up. We need more than circumstantial evidence."

I resisted the urge to pound the table. He was my partner, not my assistant.

"I'll talk to her," Madeleine volunteered. "It's a good way to get intel, right? You just have to ask the right questions."

As if she had broken through a force field, I suddenly noticed the clanking of lunch trays and the chatter of conversations around us. Our table was filling up. March and CindeeRae looked from me to Madeleine, their eyes bunching at me.

"What kind of questions?" I asked.

"Because you can't give us away," CindeeRae said. "That would blow the whole operation."

"Trust me." Madeline's fists pushed into her hips. "I've got this."

"Riiiiiiight . . ." March said, sneering just a little.

Madeleine smirked at him before heading back to her own lunch table, and I smiled. Just one week ago, our little team couldn't have survived lunch hour together, but look at us now, working together—kind of—on a serious rescue mission.

CindeeRae, March, and I huddled by the drinking fountain outside music class while kids left for math. Madeleine stood in the middle of the room, waiting for Mrs. Hewitt to gather all the sheets of music from where we had stacked them at the end of the risers.

"How are you doing, Madeleine?" she asked when she noticed Madeleine shifting from one foot to the other.

"I'm very sad," Madeline said, frowning.

I rolled my eyes. We should have let CindeeRae, a real professional, handle this. Conniving or not, Madeleine Brown was no *Annie* star.

"What's wrong, Madeleine?" Mrs. Hewitt set the music down on the piano and led Madeleine to the risers. "Is there something I can help you with?"

Madeleine sat down and then collapsed into a heap on her lap, her arms shielding her face. "The Denver Dognapper stole Lenny, my beautiful collie, from Sleepy Hollow the night before Halloween."

Mrs. Hewitt put her arm on Madeleine's shoulders and cooed, "I'm so sorry, sweetheart."

Madeleine snapped up, knocking Mrs. Hewitt's arm away. "Why are *you* sorry?"

"What do you mean, dear?"

"Do *you* feel bad about the missing dogs?" she asked.

"Me?" Mrs. Hewitt tilted her head to the side, looking nervous. "Why do you ask?" Maybe Madeleine *did* know what she was doing.

"Because they're dogs and they're missing. Duh! It's not rocket science."

"Oh no," I muttered. Madeleine was going off script.

Mrs. Hewitt patted Madeleine's back as CindeeRae snuck down the side of the classroom toward the teacher's desk. March elbowed me, his eyes wide as he watched her. We were going to have a long talk about sticking to mission protocol.

"Oh, sweetheart," Mrs. Hewitt said to Madeleine, like she was calculating the answer to a tricky math problem in her head. "Of course I feel bad about the missing dogs."

"I knew it," Madeleine said just as CindeeRae snatched something from inside a book on Mrs. Hewitt's desk and scurried back to us.

"Abort, abort," March whispered.

"Madeleine," I called into the room from the doorway. "We're going to be late."

Madeleine glared at me over her shoulder before turning back to Mrs. Hewitt, who smiled at us. As Madeleine walked away, she made the peace sign, pointed at her own two eyes, and then turned the fingers back on Mrs. Hewitt.

Mrs. Hewitt called after her, "Madeleine, honey, are you sure you're okay?"

"She's the one," Madeleine whispered as she walked past us, and we shuffled to keep up with her.

"She's right," CindeeRae said, flashing the paper she had taken from Mrs. Hewitt's desk. It was a receipt from the same King Soopers that Crowley had bought his fifteen bags from, only for two cheaper bags.

"I don't know," March said. "It could be for Pickles."

"But it's the only clue we have," Madeleine said. "Plus, did you hear her? She admitted she feels guilty about the missing dogs."

"She feels bad," March clarified. "*Bad* is different from *guilty*."

"We only have one more night." I lowered my voice as we started up the crowded stairway to our classrooms. "And no other clues."

"Let's meet at my house after school." March stopped on the landing, leaning into our huddle. "We need to talk this out before we do anything else."

Mom was waiting at my bus stop. She wore a long puffer jacket the color of cranberries, the fur-trimmed hood pulled over her head even though it wasn't snowing. She asked questions nonstop as we walked home through our neighborhood: How was school? Did I eat all my lunch? Did I remember to put my homework folder in my backpack? Was there another safety assembly today? Was I feeling any better about Genki? Was I sad or afraid?

I gave her yes and no answers.

Then she asked the big question she had been leading up to. "Why did you lie to us about Mr. Crowley? That's just not like you, Kazu." All those ordinary questions followed by a whammy.

Mom's super-sense was better than a lie detector any day of the week. I decided to stick as close to the truth as possible without giving away any big clues.

"I was afraid to tell the Tanners it was my fault Barkley went missing. I guess I wanted to blame someone else so they wouldn't hate me."

"By making up the story about finding Barkley's collar in the garbage can?"

If I told Mom the truth, she would work at me until I caved and shared everything I knew. I couldn't put Genki in danger like that.

I nodded.

Mom didn't respond, and the only noise I could hear was the *shush, shush* of her puffer jacket. Hopefully, when this was all over, she would still want me to be her assistant in designing the new spy and sleuthing exhibition at the exploration museum. "It took a lot of courage to be honest, Kazuko." She wrapped an arm around my shoulder. "Now we can all stand back and let the police do their job and bring Genki home."

That one sentence wound around my heart and made my chest ache. I told myself that, ultimately, we were helping the police do their job. Maybe when we discovered the location of doggie-holding headquarters, we could finally share all our clues with them, and they could bring our puppies back.

As we rounded the corner toward our house, a DineWise van pulled in across the street. Mrs. White stood at the edge of her driveway, where she used her cane to motion the vehicle into her tidy garage. As we got closer, she waved at us, her arm circling her side like a giant bird trying to redirect its course.

I stopped walking, staring at the DineWise van disappearing into Mrs. White's garage. Mom continued to walk, her arms still rustling against the jacket.

WITHE = WHITE. No extra *T*.

I remembered our conversation from when I pulled her weeds a month ago. Mrs. White needed money to open a nice little store selling old-people gadgets— the kind of money you could make selling dogs in a dognapping ring. The store she opened would be named after her husband Nile: Seenile Gizmos. That was the name of a local company depositing money into Crowley's account.

"Earth to Kazuko Jones!" Mom stood at the base of our walkway, arms outstretched. "Hello?"

"Coming," I said, running past her and into the house.

I had to tell the team.

CHAPTER FORTY-ONE

I rushed to my room and grabbed the Zoo Crew packs with all the supplies from our last mission. My stomach somersaulted and my eyes stung.

"Kazu?" Mom stood in my doorway, hands on hips. "What are you doing?"

I knelt on the floor in front of my closet, holding the pack in my hands. I leaned back onto my heels to look up at her. "I'm gathering some stuff for an assignment."

"What assignment?"

I stirred my hand inside the pack, thinking. "It's a show-and-tell thing. Mrs. Thomas wants us to make a package of everything we'd take to a deserted island."

"Oh?" She raised her eyebrows and stepped closer. "What would you take?"

I pulled out the kazoo. "This?" I reached back inside and pulled out the pocketknife. "And this? Because, survival?"

She looked at me.

"That's all I have so far," I said.

"What about a book? You'd need something to keep yourself occupied."

"I can only take five things, and one of them will be a box of Froot Loops."

"That leaves two more."

"And a rain jacket and a magnifying glass, to build a fire. There's no room for books." I couldn't believe I was arguing about an imaginary assignment.

"You don't even want a picture of your family?"

"All right! I'll trade the magnifying glass for a family portrait, because that'll keep me warm at night."

Mom started to say something and then stopped. Her face softened, and she said, "You're right, Kazu. You've got this."

I nodded, so shocked I couldn't think of anything to say.

Then she asked, "Would you like to go to the Golden Buckle for dinner tonight?"

My parents were super good at knowing how to comfort me, but I needed to meet the gang at March's house to plan tonight's mission, Operation: Take Down Mrs. White.

"Mom, I can't tonight," I said. "We're all meeting at March's house to work on this assignment. Can we go tomorrow night?"

Mom chewed on her bottom lip before responding. "Of course. What would you like me to make you for dinner tonight, then?"

"Katsudon." Next to baked manicotti, it was my favorite: a Japanese dish with a fried pork cutlet on a bed of rice soaking in an amazing soupy sauce with a scrambled egg on top.

Mom nodded. "You got it."

I realized I just may have requested my last meal.

March had unrolled a bolt of butcher paper across the floor, from the window to his closet. "I thought we could map out our plan here." He gestured to the floor, where two marker packets and a big box of crayons aligned perfectly with the border of the paper.

"But we haven't even decided where we're going yet." Madeleine had been sitting at the desk but stood to approach me and CindeeRae on the bottom bunk of March's bed.

"I just told you," I said. "Crowley's partner is Mrs. White, my neighbor, *not* Mrs. Hewitt."

Madeleine folded her arms and huffed at me. "*You* think so, but there were just as many clues pointing to Mrs. Hewitt."

March, who hadn't been convinced that our music teacher was the dognapping mastermind in the first place, had quickly agreed with me in naming Mrs. White our primary suspect. I looked to CindeeRae for support.

She shrugged.

"What?" I said. "Mrs. White fits the code perfectly. No extra *T*."

"I know." CindeeRae picked at the knee of her jeans, not meeting my eyes. "But just this afternoon you thought Hewitt fit the code perfectly. And what about the receipt?"

March jumped in. "It was only for two bags of dog food, and they were cheaper than the ones on Crowley's receipt, probably because the bags were smaller. You don't buy two small bags of dog food when you're feeding lots of dogs. Plus, it was probably for her dog, Pickles."

"That's another clue." Madeleine held up two fingers. "She was at Sleepy Hollow the night Lenny was taken."

"The *Processes and Procedures* document proves that Crowley and WITHE do different things. Taking the dogs isn't WITHE's job." I stood and stepped across the butcher paper to face Madeleine down. "She holds the dogs, and Crowley takes them."

That piece of information deflated Madeleine a bit, and she dropped her counting fingers and crossed her arms over her chest again.

"That's true," CindeeRae agreed from her perch on March's bed.

"And don't forget the payment Crowley gets from Seenile Gizmos," I said, certain no one could argue with that. "Mrs. White's husband's name was Nile, and she wants to start a business selling gadgets for old people. That's a pretty solid connection between Crowley and White. Not to mention the regular DineWise deliveries inside her closed garage."

We could hear March's brothers banging around the next room, fighting over something called a *flubber-blaster*.

"Should we take a vote?" March asked.

CindeeRae nodded and Madeleine dropped her arms to her sides.

"All those in favor of Mission: Take Down Mrs. White, raise your hands."

March, CindeeRae, and I raised our hands. Madeleine let out a slow breath, rolled her eyes to the ceiling, and raised her hand, too.

"Then it's unanimous!" I tried to high-five Madeleine, but she kept both arms stiff at her sides.

"You better be right," she said. "Because there's no time for mistakes."

CHAPTER FORTY-TWO

By the time we had finished planning the mission, the butcher paper looked like a giant comic book panel.

It started with a diagram of Mrs. White's house, arrows pointing to the front door, the garage door, and the keypad for the security code.

We knew that Crowley didn't bring the dogs inside his house, but because the processes and procedures document said WITHE held them for seventy-two hours, we decided the dogs must be somewhere in Mrs. White's house.

She had hired me to do lots of odd jobs inside over the last two years. I once swept the cobwebs from the ceiling corners in her basement. I had painted a spare room upstairs. And I had cleaned out all her kitchen cab-inets, emptying each drawer and wiping it down before applying new contact paper. I knew the inside of her house, and the only place she could hide dogs for longer periods of time without anyone noticing would be the basement: our target location.

Next to the picture of her house was a square labeled *Step One* with a close-up of the garage keypad and the code I had been entering myself for two years: 1065. We would enter through the garage to the side door.

Step's Two and Three were in the same square. In CindeeRae's swirly handwriting was a close-up of the side door with another keypad beneath a doorbell. We would run to the keypad and shut the door before Mrs. White could hear anything. Step Three: Open the door with the house key hidden above the door frame. If that didn't work, we had learned how to pick a lock for the failed mission in Crowley's garage.

I had drawn the square for Step Four, which included a map of the house's main floor, with a dotted line trav-eling from the garage through the kitchen, past the back door, and down the stairs. At the top of the landing, Madeleine would stand watch.

On Step Five, March, CindeeRae, and I would stop any potential barking by giving the dogs peanut-butter tortilla wraps—we couldn't afford to have yapping dogs foil another mission.

Step Six also took place in the basement, where we would retrieve the dogs and escape through the back door of Mrs. White's house, which Madeleine would open for us as she waited on the landing. We'd cut through the backyard to a gate at the side that opened onto my street. If we were being chased, we would run to my house, where the front door would be unlocked. If we left undetected, we would get our bikes from my backyard and go back to our homes before our parents even realized we were missing.

Like a signature, CindeeRae, Madeleine, and I had each drawn a small picture of our dogs in the bottom right-hand corner of the butcher paper.

"That looks good." I stepped back to take in the big picture and then scribbled the steps in my Sleuth Chronicle.

"We are breaking and entering." March filed his markers back into the box with a sigh.

CindeeRae patted his arm. "Think of it as hacking into her house."

I handed them their Zoo Crew packs. "It has everything from before, including a few extras."

"Extras?" March asked.

"The peanut-butter wraps, and either a lightsaber or a wand."

"Lightsaber or wand. For what?"

"Protection?" I shrugged. "I was just jamming stuff in there at the end."

March rolled up the butcher paper and folded it to the size of a newspaper, cramming it into his pack. We all watched until he was finally able to work the zipper closed, sighing loudly before realizing we had been watching him the whole time. He blushed.

"So we meet at my place, midnight," I said.

They all nodded like everything we had just planned was perfectly reasonable.

CHAPTER FORTY-THREE

We stood in the shadow of the eaves over Mrs. White's garage, huddled around the keypad. We had just walked our bikes into my backyard, shut the gate, and sneaked to Mrs. White's. Even though we were just across the street from where my parents slept, it felt as if we were in a foreign land.

I hadn't considered how loud the garage door might be when activated this late at night. If Mrs. White woke up before we even got inside, everything would be ruined. I looked around. It was just after midnight and the neighborhood was dark. Even though the moon was a sliver, Mrs. White's baby-blue house seemed to glow. A car could drive down our street any second and see a four-kid outline against the house like a giant arrow.

I pulled the headlamp over my hoodie, clicked it on, and took a deep breath as I began pressing numbers: 1065—the month and year of Mrs. White's wedding. I waited a beat to press five, almost long enough for the lights on the keypad to flash red for failure. But then I thought of Genki cowering in the basement, and I pushed my thumb hard in the center of the pad before pressing the up arrow to open the door. Luckily Mrs. White maintained everything on her property with exactness, and the garage opened silently. Allen, the handyman, had probably oiled the rails this week.

The opening of the garage door triggered the light inside, and I ran to the keypad to turn it off and reverse the door, waving March, CindeeRae, and Madeleine over as it closed. We crouched by her back steps as the garage door creaked toward the pavement, my breathing the only thing I could hear. After a length of silence, and only when I was certain Mrs. White hadn't been awakened, I grabbed the house key she hid atop the door frame and pulled off my backpack. I dropped the headlamp inside and reached for the small flashlight.

I turned to them and asked, "Are you ready?"

CindeeRae's face looked pale against the black beanie she wore. When she nodded, I realized her crooked headlamp shone on her face, making her eye sockets all dark and creepy. Madeleine had opted for a dark red bandanna tied over her long braids, while March wore his own beanie, for Gryffindor, with a pom-pom on the top, the ball motionless.

"Are you sure about this, Kazu?" He covered his headlamp with his fingers so the light wouldn't blind me. "This could be really bad if we get caught."

"I've got to save Genki," I whispered, and CindeeRae nodded. "But I would understand if you decided to guard the perimeter instead and let my parents know if we don't come out."

"Isn't that Madeleine's job?"

"Kinda." I shrugged. She would actually be in the house with us, though, and it couldn't hurt to have two people on lookout.

"Okay," he said. "I'm coming."

I unlocked the door and pushed it open. The lights on the main floor were off, so I turned on the flashlight and bounced the beam around Mrs. White's living room. The house looked like a movie set from the seventies—the carpet, furniture, and wallpaper were old but looked new, as if no one had been allowed to move around inside.

We walked past the living room and through the kitchen, where a back door marked the top of the basement stairs: Madeleine's mark.

Feeling like Genki's escape was moments away, I tiptoed down the stairs as if each step contained an invisible booby trap. March and CindeeRae held back, and when I reached the bottom I had to wait for them to catch up.

Moonlight shone through the window on the landing. I caught Madeleine's eye and flashed her a thumbs-up, which she returned.

March, CindeeRae, and I reached into our packs and pulled out two wraps each. When I touched the doorknob, I thought I heard Genki's whimper. I swung it wide.

The basement was dark, but I could see the walls were covered with bumpy foam, and the back corner of the room was filled with bags and bags of dog food. Kennels lined the walls, but only a handful were occupied. The room exploded with barking, and dogs lurched at their kennel gates. The three of us rushed to deliver peanut-butter wraps to each of the kennels, and the barking slowly quieted. My chest tightened. Had we been fast enough?

Across the room I saw Genki in the last crate on the right, and my heart sped up. When he saw me, he did the little tapping dance he does when waiting to be fed, his tail beating the back of the kennel. I ran to him and dropped a wrap through the top of his crate, but he ignored it. I pushed my palms into the wires, and Genki licked my fingers.

From behind, I heard CindeeRae yelp, and a kennel door slam. I started to open the latch when March hollered in my ear, and as I turned I saw him fall to the floor, his eyes wide. "Run," he screamed, but when I took a step toward him I was pushed down, too, my knees knocking on the concrete.

Mrs. White loomed above, her face grouchy, like when I accidentally flattened her tulips with the Sunday paper. She pinched Madeleine's shoulders with craggy fingers and pushed her into another kennel. Madeleine's cheeks were wet. "I thought I heard Lenny, so I followed you all downstairs. I'm sorry."

Mrs. White snapped the padlock shut.

CHAPTER FORTY-FOUR

I scrambled backward with March, pedaling my legs against the concrete floor. Mrs. White held out her cane, resting the end of it on my shoulder.

"Kazuko Jones," she said. "Always curious. Always industrious."

CindeeRae was weeping across the room, where she hunched in a kennel with a padlock on the door. I was so distracted with finding Genki, I hadn't even heard Mrs. White come downstairs.

She snapped her fingers to get my attention. "When I started this whole project, I had hoped I'd get Seenile Gizmos up and running by the time you were old enough to work the register. You're a dream employee, except for that darned nosiness. And now, you may have ruined everything." With the cane she motioned at the largest kennel in the room. I looked at March. The two of us could knock Mrs. White down and escape, but then we'd be leaving CindeeRae, Madeleine, and Genki behind. March studied the floor, his eyes moving back and forth like he was ready to slip into a panic attack. *We're in this together*, I thought. So I followed my best friend inside the kennel, and Mrs. White closed the latch and hung a padlock from the gate.

Mrs. White dropped a bedazzled phone into the pocket of her bathrobe, and then rubbed her hands together like she had pulled a weed from her garden and needed to brush the dirt from her fingers. So much for having someone on lookout.

"Let's all hope you three don't end up like Loralee Sanders." She turned around, and, without looking back, walked toward the stairs and slammed the door behind her.

CindeeRae had calmed down, but Madeleine was still crying in her kennel, even after the dogs had calmed down and curled inside their cages. All except Genki, who whimpered and pawed at his metal crate no matter what I said to soothe him.

The basement was dark, the light from a back

bathroom casting a shadow of the kennels onto the wall. My back was to the corner, the metal wiring biting into my skin and making me sore. March sat cross-legged next to me. His knees buckled at his shoulders, making him look like a frog.

"Now what do we do?" he asked.

I pulled the Gryffindor beanie from his head because he looked ridiculous. "I don't know. We hadn't planned for the possibility of being caged with the dogs. Besides, aren't you the brainiac of this operation?"

"There's nothing digital about breaking out of here."

I threw my head back, and it banged on the kennel.

"Who's Loralee Sanders?" March asked.

"What do you mean?" I remembered Mrs. White telling me about the papergirl who got disappeared by some wackadoodle while collecting payment for the paper. I shivered involuntarily.

"Mrs. White said something about Loralee Sanders." He leaned forward to study my face. "You *do* know, Kazuko Jones. I can tell."

My sigh came out in a long shudder. Telling the others about Loralee Sanders would freak them out. No, it would make them Barkley-level afraid—they might roll over and wet their kennels.

March glared at me.

"Okay, okay," I said. "She was this papergirl who

disappeared more than twenty years ago after collecting money from some crazy guy on her route."

"What?" March said, his voice squeaky.

"It doesn't matter," I said to him, and then called across the room. "Madeleine, you've got to snap out of it. We have to get out of here."

Madeleine was drawn into a ball, her knees pulled to her chest. She mumbled something, her words muffled by the barricade her arms made around her head.

"What?" March and I asked.

She looked up. "I was hoping Lenny would still be here."

March and I looked around. Some of the kennels were empty, and some of them had two dogs inside. None of them had Lobster or Lenny. Madeleine ducked her head back behind the barricade while CindeeRae hooked her fingers through the kennel wires.

"I'm sorry, Madeleine," March said. "I thought you knew they had probably already sent Lenny somewhere; it's been more than seventy-two hours. But once the police know Mr. Crowley and Mrs. White are the dognappers, they'll be able to track down all the missing dogs."

CindeeRae said, "How are they going to find out? You heard her—Mrs. White wants to disappear us like Loralee Sanders."

March looked at me as if he suddenly realized we were locked in a doggie kennel with two criminals deciding our fate. "She's right. They're gonna drop us into a well or something. If they don't, we'll rat them out, and they'll be arrested. No dognapping empire for either of them."

"Calm down," I said.

March was breathing too fast. He began to rock back and forth, his leg rolling over my fingers each time he fell forward.

"Count to ten, slowly," I said. I had seen this in a movie before—March was hypervasculating or something. "You're going to pass out if you don't slow down."

March stopped rocking and unfolded his body, his back resting on the kennel and his feet touching the door. He was still too big to stretch his legs out, and they bent at the knee.

"They can't do anything to us if we escape first," I said.

"How are we going to escape?" CindeeRae asked. "She's pacing up there, grumbling about how we've ruined everything. Whatever they do, it'll be before tomorrow morning when all our parents realize we're missing. Until then, she's not going to sleep or step out for coffee."

I looked from March to CindeeRae to Madeleine, all of them staring me down. CindeeRae was right, but if we sat down here until the dognappers made a move, we'd never get away.

"Let's wait awhile and see if the pacing stops," I said. "She doesn't expect us to get out of the kennels, so if she goes to the back of the house, we could sneak out without her even knowing. Until then, I'll pick our locks, and we'll be ready to make a run for it, no matter what happens."

CHAPTER FORTY-FIVE

I pulled out my Zoo Crew pack and dumped everything onto the doggie bed cushioning at the bottom of the kennel. The night we had planned to break into Crowley's house to save Genki, we had watched a YouTube video on lock-picking a handful of times and even tried it on my back door. It had taken a while, but the lock's core had finally clicked, and the door popped open. I hoped a padlock worked the same as a door lock.

Realizing what I was doing, March pulled his headlamp from where it lay next to his Gryffindor beanie, and snapped it into place on his forehead. We both knelt next to the kennel door, and I pulled the padlock as close to me as possible. March held it in place and focused the beam of his headlamp on the keyhole while I went to work.

One bobby pin was bent in half and acted as the lever I would use to put pressure on the lock and eventually open it. The other was bent straight with a little hook on the end, the tool I would use to open each pin in the locking mechanism.

I pushed the lever into the lock, holding it down and to the left. I shoved the pick above it and began the slow work of listening as I lifted each of the five lock pins. While some of them popped up easily, some were stuck in place and required jiggling. I got to the fourth pin when I lost my hold on the pick, and they all snapped down.

"Remember—slow, deep breaths," March whispered, his mouth at my ear, and only then did I hear my quick and raspy breathing. It filled the basement and sounded like a wounded animal. I pulled the tools from the lock and took slow, deep breaths with my eyes closed until I calmed down.

"Do you want me to try?" March asked.

I shook my head, and March returned the beam of his headlamp to the padlock. The clicking of pins as they were pushed into place sounded like money dropping into a coin purse—the happiest of sounds. A chill traveled down my back as the final pin clicked into place and the padlock dropped open.

After picking one padlock, the rest were easy. We crouched by Genki's after releasing him and waited for the noise upstairs to stop. Like a frenzied melody, the pacing slowly subsided and was replaced by silence.

"When should we leave?" March breathed.

"It's pretty quiet right now," CindeeRae whispered.

I turned my ear toward the ceiling, as if that might help us know what Mrs. White was doing. The house creaked as it settled, and our breathing synced as we waited.

The phone rang, a low guttural sound that made us jump. We heard Mrs. White patter across the house to the spot above the stairs.

"Hello?" A short pause followed without sound.

Her voice was muffled as she spoke, but I could have sworn I heard her say "get rid of them."

"Oh no," I murmured. "They're going to come down here."

Mrs. White walked across the kitchen floor, and I imagined her pulling the long cord behind her. She could probably go to the bathroom and still talk on the phone, the cord's slack pooling in the hallway.

"Thirty minutes? I'll be ready. . . ."

She paced some more, her footfalls faster, heavier.

Then, suddenly, she was pounding down the stairs toward us. Without thinking, I pulled a red lightsaber from my Zoo Crew pack.

The basement door opened and light from the stairwell flooded behind Mrs. White's stocky body, creating an ominous silhouette and trapping us in the back of the room. She held the phone in one outstretched hand and her cane in the other. Her robe was open, revealing an oversize sweatshirt that hung right above her knees, BEST GRANDMA printed across her chest. A low growl rumbled from the base of Genki's throat as Mrs. White yelled into the phone. "They got out. Get over here. NOW!"

I stood and took a couple steps toward her, and Genki followed while March and CindeeRae hung back. The dogs in their kennels began to bark again, and I wished we'd had time to release them all to cause a distraction.

She dropped the receiver. The springy cord pulled it from the air, and I heard it hit the stairs out of sight.

"Mr. Crowley's on his way," she said. "He was on his cell phone in the truck. He'll be here any minute."

Catching my gaze, she pointed her cane at us. My throat tightened, making it hard to breathe.

"Guys," I screamed. "Go out the back door!"

I rushed forward, waving the red lightsaber back and forth like a sword. Genki sped ahead of me, and, like he had trained for this one moment his entire life, backed Mrs. White against the wall, his teeth bared like a frothing were-monster. March, CindeeRae, and Madeleine bolted up the stairs behind us.

Mrs. White stabbed at Genki with the cane, and he yelped as his back leg buckled.

"You are a very mean old lady!" I swung the lightsaber at her leg and it bent in half, taking a second to spring back into place. Mrs. White tried to reach for the plastic, swinging both hands and dropping her cane.

"The door's jammed!" March called down the stairs, distracting Mrs. White as Genki recovered. He stood with his back arched, barking so loudly my ears hurt. The other dogs barked even louder, and soon the entire basement was throbbing with the noise.

I swung the lightsaber at Mrs. White's shoulder, and this time the plastic stayed bent. She jolted, banging her head against the wall and bending to grab her cane from the ground. I beat her to it and swatted at her feet; she lost her balance and tumbled to the ground.

"Go to the garage," I yelled to March as I ran up the stairs, Genki following behind me.

"You won't get away," Mrs. White called after me. "It never takes him long to get here."

Sure enough, as soon as we entered the garage, the large door began to crank open, activated by a remote outside. With Mrs. White behind us and Crowley ahead, we had nowhere to go.

CHAPTER FORTY-SIX

The beams from the DineWise van slowly filled the garage as the door rose. I hit the button on the keypad, which paused it a foot above the cement floor, and I ran to the one window in the garage across from the door. I stood on my tiptoes and slammed the base of the lightsaber into the window, shattering it.

"What are you doing?" March called at me, his voice shaking.

"Hide behind the garbage cans!" I yelled back as the garage door was activated again, opening wider. I slid next to March, CindeeRae, and Madeleine, and pulled Genki down to the floor, his tail still wagging. "Quiet!" I commanded Genki as the garage door reached the half-way point, and light from the truck flooded the garage.

We huddled in the shadows of the three garbage cans, between an upright freezer and Mrs. White's gardening tools hanging from hooks on the wall. I didn't think Crowley would be able to see us, but that was only if he wasn't searching. He shut the garage door before getting out of the truck and rushing into the house without even glancing around the garage.

"Hurry, hurry, hurry," I mumbled at them as I stood and swung open the lid on the garbage can next to the house steps. I pulled Genki to the top step and held the can at an angle for him. "Come!" I said as I pointed inside. Like we were playing Simon Says, March, CindeeRae, and Madeleine followed my commands and crowded into garbage cans.

The dark room shook like an earthquake. I jolted, feeling the walls around me tight like a coffin, and realized Genki was curved around my feet, his head resting awkwardly on the hook of my heel. Then I remembered that I was hunched over in Mrs. White's garbage can, and the rumbling was probably Allen pushing her trash to the curb.

I must have dozed off after Crowley came. He had gone into the house, leaving the door open a crack, so we could hear his angry conversation with Mrs. White.

Then he tore back into the garage, noticed the broken glass, and ran out back, trying to follow our trail out the window and through the neighborhood. I assumed he hoped to catch us before we found cover or made it back to our families.

His frustrated return was followed by more commotion as Crowley and Mrs. White loaded the truck and drove away. We whispered back and forth for a bit, and decided the safest place was in the garbage cans; I was certain they would come back for the dogs and catch us all as we tried to flee. I must have fallen asleep soon after, no longer bothered by the smell of the spoiled DineWise tins and orange peels I had used to cover Genki and me.

My garbage can stopped, and I listened as Allen pushed the other cans to the curb. When I heard his car pull away, I rocked my bin back and forth until it toppled over. I pushed the lid open, the early morning light blinding me as Genki tentatively pushed his way out. March's eyes peeked from under his lid.

I laughed at the smudge of dirt on his fingers, which hung over the can's rim. "We did it," I whispered, still afraid someone might hear us. "Mission accomplished!"

The lid of the last can flew back, and CindeeRae and Madeleine sprang up like a two-headed jack-in-the-box.

"We're alive!" Madeleine cried.

Genki circled me a couple times before crossing the street to our house. Two police cars and one black SUV were parked at the curb, and Detective Hawthorne's hulking back blocked all the light in the doorway.

I grabbed March's arms and pulled him from the garbage can, which toppled onto Mrs. White's front yard. CindeeRae and Madeleine had already scrambled from their bin, which had been halfway full of recyclables, and the plastic bottles and tin cans clanked onto the street. Detective Hawthorne turned toward the noise. Mom pushed past him and darted across the yard in her bare feet, even though the grass was crunchy with frost.

"Kazuko?" She stopped on the road and looked at me. "Kazu?" she said again, louder this time.

"Mom," I said, and ran to her, leaving March in the frozen grass. She knelt and hugged me, squeezing the air from my chest. Genki jumped up on us, barking for attention. When she finally let go, she held me at arm's length, searching my face. "Are you okay?"

I nodded my head, and she hugged me again, her tears wetting my cheek. I inhaled the scent of yuzu, Mom's Japanese bath salts that smelled like tangerines, and knew everything would finally be okay.

CHAPTER FORTY-SEVEN

March, CindeeRae, and I were racing our bikes, standing on our pedals to go faster. The cold air bit at my bare fingers, and I sped up to try to pull ahead of March. The sun shone bright on Thanksgiving Day in Denver, Colorado, although the temperature was still cold enough for snow. We pedaled down the park road and past Pioneer Village, where the tools and other props had already been taken inside for winter. Genki pounded the pavement next to me, his jowls flapping in the wind and his mouth open in a big grin. March had left Hopper at home, but CindeeRae pulled Lobster along on a long leash, and it looked like the spinning wheels made her dog forget how to run in a straight line.

"Eat my dust!" March yelled as I passed, my pedal nearly hitting his wheel as I swerved around him.

"Suckah!" I said, laughing.

"Wait up," CindeeRae called after us, and I sat down on my bike seat and held my legs out so my pedals could spin without my feet.

The sound of our bikes hummed in my ears, and I threw my head back and hollered. Now that everything had been solved—with Crowley and White in jail—we were free to ride around the park, as long as we returned to March's house in time for pie. The emergency cell phone bobbed up and down in my back pocket as I rode.

By the time Allen had pushed our garbage cans to the curb that morning, Mrs. White and Crowley were long gone, headed to his sister-in-law's cabin in Greybull, Wyoming. It didn't take long for Detective Hawthorne to find the location, the address popping up as the most recently searched item on Crowley's home computer. On Mrs. White's computer they found a coded spreadsheet listing each dog that had been taken and where they had been sent. Within a week, they had decoded the document, and all the dogs had been located and returned to their happy humans, including Lenny, Lobster, and Barkley, just in time to welcome his new baby sister. With our case closed, Madeleine didn't have much of a reason to talk to us at school anymore, but she still smiled every time she passed me in the hall.

The four of us spent approximately twenty-six hours feeling kinda famous after the *Denver Chronicle* ran an article about our keen detecting skills. But the next day they ran an update detailing how our nosiness had gotten us into a slew of trouble, including confrontations with both the dogfighters and the dognappers, which could have cost us our lives. Even though we were minors and the paper legally couldn't include our names, everyone at Lincoln Elementary School knew who we were and started calling us the Granny Busters.

Our parents were proud until Detective Hawthorne debriefed us in his cubicle, and they realized how many botched missions we had voluntarily engaged in. "But our last one was successful," I had argued as Mom pinched my earlobe. "One out of four isn't a bad record for beginners."

Detective Hawthorne tossed his pen onto his desk and shook his head. "Promise me you four will stay out of trouble from now on. Leave crime-solving to the professionals, okay?"

We nodded, and he handed the Sleuth Chronicle back to me. Mom had surrendered it when they discovered I was missing, hoping it might give them information on our whereabouts. Unfortunately, it only tipped them off to my Hero Complex, which, if I was being honest, was still alive and kicking.

In addition to being grounded for a few weeks, we

all had to do community service for twenty hours each at the Denver Police Department's K-9 unit and promise Detective Hawthorne we would never meddle in an open investigation again. I had been sure to clarify that detecting was fine, as long as we weren't illegal about it. He then made us each write a paper detailing everything we did on the dognapper case that was illegal or obstructive. March, CindeeRae, and Madeleine had not been happy about that extra assignment. I had found it very enlightening.

Mom had been busy preparing the Exhibition of Espionage and Sleuthing this past month, and CindeeRae, March, and I had already been to the museum twice to help her build the set. The exhibition would be launched in January, and Mom promised I could participate in the big party she would throw on opening day. Aside from being angry at all the dangerous detecting we had done, Mom had admitted, grudgingly, that I had proven myself rather clever. If all that cleverness could just be legal from now on, she'd be grateful, thank you very much.

As we sped down the shady path behind Pioneer Village, I saw a man step from the blacksmith cabin, a duffel bag in his hand. The navy bag said SMITHEN on the side, and from the unzipped top I could see what looked like stacks of bills lining the inside. We turned the corner where a cement wall hid the museum, and I skidded to a stop.

"What are you doing?" March stopped his bike.

CindeeRae caught up as I pulled my new iPad from my bike basket: Sleuth Chronicle 2.0.

"Taking notes," I said, recording everything I had seen.

"No, no, no, no," March said, snapping the cover shut on my fingers. "I know what you're doing, and I'm not going to let it happen."

CindeeRae nodded in agreement.

I shrugged, pulling my iPad away and setting it back in my bike basket. "Whatever, Granny Busters."

"Ha," March said, launching his bike ahead of mine. "Race you both home?"

"You don't stand a chance!" I yelled, cycling so fast my feet nearly spun off the pedals.

"Wait up!" CindeeRae trailed behind us, Lobster sniffing at Genki, who ran by her side.

We turned onto Honeysuckle and weaved back and forth across the road, cars tucked neatly into driveways on the quiet holiday. It wouldn't be long before a Colorado winter quarantined us all, and I would have nothing to do but study my SleuthPad and practice saving the world.

Acknowledgments

To me, writing fiction in any capacity is an act of faith. But especially before you have an agent or a book deal. This story was written in the solitary and optimistic hours of unknowing, and materialized only with the help and encouragement of my most favorite people. Without them, *Kazu Jones and the Denver Dognappers* never would have been published.

My senior year high school English teacher, Mrs. Johansen, was the first person to ever encourage me to write, by scrawling "You should become an author" at the top of a personal essay. Before that, I had never considered creative writing as a thing I could do.

Following her kind words, I found myself enrolling in every creative writing class I could find at college (go, BYU-Hawaii Seasiders!), which is where I found my most treasured mentor, Chris Crowe. In graduate school, he became my thesis chair and my champion, and without his positive reinforcement I wouldn't be here.

After convincing myself to finally get serious about writing, I stumbled upon the Snake River Writers, a local writing group that introduced me to critique partners, conferences, and a rowdy community of fun and encouraging human beings. Special thanks to extrovert extraordinaire Gina Larsen, who ensured I didn't waste away as a sad, introverted writing hermit holed up at my kitchen counter. Other buddies from this group include Becky Bryan, Serene Heiner, Daniel Noyes, Karianne Perrenoud, Megan Clements, Carrie Snider, Maggie Decker, Jessica Wiseman, Melissa Gamble, Simone Stoumbaugh, and Melinda Erb. Thank you for being bright stars who are nothing but loving and supportive!

My Wednesday Night Writers critique group here in Idaho Falls were the first to read *Kazu Jones*, and their feedback and insight helped the manuscript level up. Extra-special thanks to Diana Shaw-Tracy, Deborah Poole, Sarah Russell, Rebecca Sanchez, Meighan Perry, and Robyn Buchanan.

It would take pages and pages to name all the attendees and presenters at the Storymakers Conference who have positively impacted me on my writing journey. Thank you, thank you, thank you.

I'm so grateful to the writing community I found online, and to my first electronic writers group, Pitch Crit Crew, especially the administrators, Aften Szymanski and Wendy Knight. And a special thanks to Aften, Cassandra Newbould, Jueneke Wong, Maura Jotner, Kimberly Johnson, Jennifer Dugan, Danielle Doolittle, Jamie Lane, Sheena Boekweg, Heather Bower, Laura Vpvp, Rachel Larsen, Erin Shakespeare Bishop, and

Shelly Brown for all your feedback on pitches, queries, chapters, and sometimes, entire manuscripts.

The writing community on Twitter is especially generous, and I marvel at all the authors who organize and promote contests and chats intended to lift and inspire fellow writers. I'm a 2016 #PitchSlam alum and am grateful to the hosts who sacrifice so much time and energy to this cause: LL McKinney, Laura Heffernan, Kimberly Vanderhorst, and Jamie Corrigan.

It was through #PitchSlam that I found my tireless agent, Carrie Pestritto, who believed in this story and found it a home. Thanks so much, Carrie! And I'd be a huge loser-pants if I didn't also thank her fabulous interns, Bea Conti and Rosiee Thor.

Laura Schreiber made my life when she invited me into the Disney Hyperion family. And together with my editor, Hannah Allaman, they saw this book for what it could become and gave me the kindest, most encouraging revision notes ever. They saw a better book than I had submitted and helped me revise it so *Kazu Jones* could come closer to its potential.

Also, Grace Hwang, what a beautiful cover! I will forever love the sassy and determined look on Kazu's face. Not to mention all the hidden puppers!

When I first started this story I mistakenly believed living in Japan for a couple years and then working as a Japanese tour guide in Hawaii had provided me with the necessary expertise to write a story about a Japanese American girl. I'm embarrassed at that ignorant assumption; it definitely had not. I'm forever grateful to Misa Sugiura, a tremendous author herself, for performing a sensitivity read and helping me recognize the cultural shortcomings in this book's draft. I'm not delusional enough to believe my revisions resulted in perfect representation, but with Misa's help, it came a lot closer. All remaining mistakes I readily accept as my own.

And of course, thanks to my mom, dad, and stepdad, who encouraged me to live my best life (and probably don't know about all the trouble I got into while out riding my bike).

The inspiration for this story came to me while driving my kids—Kaleb, Leah, and Zack—on their own paper routes years ago. While I may hate early mornings, I will always treasure those hours we spent rolling and delivering newspapers together.

When I told my husband I wanted to quit freelancing to write fiction, he didn't hesitate. "Go for it," he said, exhibiting more faith in my abilities than I had. Thank you, Michael Holyoak, for being my biggest fan before I had even completed a manuscript.

And FINALLY, when Mike and I got married, we brought together the best blended family in the history of ever, which we fondly refer to as the Belyoak Bunch. I'm grateful to be the bonus mom for four great kids: Harrison, Claire, Carma, and Greyson. In my opinion, there's nothing better for middle-grade writers than living in a home full of kids, and our seven-big crew definitely gave me a slew of material!